FIFTY SHADES OF
DORIAN GRAY

FIFTY SHADES OF DORIAN GRAY

Oscar Wilde & Nicole Audrey Spector

Skyhorse Publishing

Skyhorse Publishing books may be purchased in bulk at special discounts for sales promotion, corporate gifts, fund-raising, or educational purposes. Special editions can also be created to specifications. For details, contact the Special Sales Department, Skyhorse Publishing, 307 West 36th Street, 11th Floor, New York, NY 10018 or info@skyhorsepublishing.com.

Skyhorse® and Skyhorse Publishing® are registered trademarks of Skyhorse Publishing, Inc.®, a Delaware corporation.

www.skyhorsepublishing.com

10 9 8 7 6 5 4 3 2 1

iSBN: 978-1- 62087-507-0

Printed in the United States of America

Table of Contents

CHAPTER I

The studio was filled with the rich odor of roses, and when the light summer wind stirred amid the trees of the garden, there came through the open door the heavy scent of lilac, or the more delicate perfume of the pink-flowering thorn. The soft breeze, infused with scent, tickled Rosemary Hall's neck, stirring the fine hairs on her nape.

It was certainly peculiar, she thought, this new awareness of feeling in her body. Even painting felt different. It was no longer just a preoccupation of mind and coordination, but a physical experience. The wetted brush was as sentient as her hand itself, and when it touched the canvas, her body stirred as if coming to life with each careful stroke.

And the daydreams she was having . . . oh, but at least those she could blink away. The dreams at night were the worst. They weren't nightmares, no—anything but, really—yet they left her deeply unsettled. Night after night, she awoke in a feverish sweat, her hips writhing on their own accord, the bed sheet coiled in a ball and clenched between her legs. It was so . . . real. Like he'd really been there. Drenched in sweat, she felt his phantom kisses linger on her cheeks. *Wherever were those dreams coming from?* Rosemary wondered. She avoided the answer. This was no time to get carried away with lust, she told herself, blushing as the word crossed her mind—a quick scurry across, then back into her subconscious.

Rosemary had just turned twenty years old and, having successfully shunned any prospects of marrying, had gotten her father to quiet on the matter. At least he was pleased with her achievements as a painter. Even her admirers were slowly deserting her. Some, like the incorrigible Buckley Brinsmead, for instance, were giving up after years of heated pursuit. It was a relief to be alone, unbothered, so that she could focus wholly on her passion. Hers would be an independent life revolving around artistic goals and nothing else. *Yes*, she thought, biting her lower lip. She would have to keep telling herself this.

From the corner of the divan of Persian saddle-bags, watching Rosemary with her signature inscrutable expression, perched Helen Wotton. She was, as always, smoking an opium-tainted cigarette.

Rosemary stepped back from the easel so Helen could get a full look at the painting and felt relief as soon as she broke contact with the canvas. She needed to get away from that tall, looming thing. Hunger seized her with a sudden urgency, and she realized she'd had only half a biscuit to eat that day. *Oh, he would be so mad if he knew that was all she'd eaten . . . Was it because he cared about her or because he just wanted to be in control?* Rosemary silently scolded herself for even wondering. She needed a break; her back was tight and knotted, and her hands felt stiff as boards and filled with a numbing ether.

"So this is it?" Helen asked. "This is the masterpiece?"

Surprisingly, there was no sarcasm in Helen's voice. Her eyes flickered with amusement as she appraised the full-length portrait of the exquisitely beautiful young man.

"Nice and big," she said to Rosemary, turning to her with a near smile.

Rosemary nodded and laughed with embarrassment.

"It's may be the biggest canvas I've ever used," confessed Rosemary in a hushed voice.

"Well, your biggest or not, it's certainly your best work yet," said Helen. "But what's really curious to me is that it may also be nature's best work—the young man, that is."

Rosemary nodded and tried to look particularly serious, but was distracted. An image of last night's dream flitted through her mind, forcing her to close her thighs to suppress the sudden ache between them. In the dream, he'd been on top of her, clutching her from behind, pushing her into the mattress, holding her hair like a strap as he thrust into her. She'd never felt a man inside her before, and expected it would be quite painful, but in the dream there was only excitement and build and a final explosion of sensation that caused her to wake with a cry.

"And quite the effect it has on you," Helen said, interrupting Rosemary's replay of the dream. "You can't even look at the greatest work of your life—the best part of *yourself*—in the eye."

Rosemary laughed and shook her head, but what Helen said was true. While Rosemary could hardly avert her gaze from the young man when he was sitting in person before her, looking at him as a painting—*her* painting—was practically unbearable. This was her best work, surely, but its effect on her was unsettling. And the man it depicted . . . oh, he was perfect then, when he walked in to her studio, just as he was now, consuming the canvas, when she could feel her own desire for him bouncing back at her, mocking her. She had not only painted his hooded gray eyes, so dark and mysterious, but had painted her own desire in them. Yes, his full-lipped, mischievous smile she'd rendered with exactitude, but there, too, was her desire, the terrifying urge for his kiss.

"You must certainly send it next year to the Grosvenor," Helen said, stubbing out her cigarette and stretching out languidly on the divan. "The Academy is too large and too vulgar. Whenever I've gone there, there have been either so many people that I haven't been able to see the pictures, which was dreadful, or so many pictures that I haven't been able to see the people, which was worse."

"I don't think I shall send it anywhere," said Rosemary. She put her head into her hands and slumped into the chair across from Helen, knocking into a lamp and catching it before it could fall and shatter.

"Please tell me you don't crash around like that before our young prince," said Helen, raising a brow at the painting and lighting another opium-tainted cigarette.

"Not that I don't love a good racket in this excruciating peace and quiet."

Rosemary was no longer listening to Helen. She was back in last night's dream. He was holding her neck tightly, almost so tightly she thought she could choke—yet she was unafraid. Her head swirled and lightened, her mind giving way to the blows of pleasure.

"No. I won't send it anywhere," she repeated.

"Why is that, my dear?" asked Helen, continuing before Rosemary could answer. "You artist types are so mad," she said, then scowled and said sarcastically, "Pardon me, only men may be mad. You, lovely lass, can only be hysterical."

"May I please explain, Helen?" asked Rosemary.

"As if I'd leave without an explanation," said Helen. "But first let me say that a portrait like this would set you far above all the other women in England. That could well put you in last place among the most wretched of men, if you're lucky."

"I know you will laugh at me," said Rosemary, "but I really can't exhibit it. I've put too much of myself into it."

On cue, Helen laughed cruelly. Her charred lungs seized the opportunity to lurch into a hacking cough. Rosemary smiled. She had never smoked a cigarette—or anything else—in her life.

"I knew you'd laugh at me, but it is quite true."

"Upon my word, Rosemary, are you in love with this Adonis? He's a Narcissus! And you, well, you have intellectual expression and all that. But beauty, real beauty, ends where intellectual expression begins. The moment one sits down to think, one becomes all nose, or all forehead, or something horrid. Take any intelligent woman you can think of—she's hideous—and you are made hideous now thinking of her. Thinking destroys the harmony of the face. Your mysterious young friend, whose name you *will* tell me, assuredly doesn't think, I can tell you that. He's a beautiful, brainless creature who should always be here in winter when we have no flowers to look at and always here in summer when we want something to chill our intelligence. Don't deceive yourself, Rosemary: Men like that don't appreciate your busy little brain."

"You don't understand me," said Rosemary. "I am not in love with him. I should be sorry to be in love with someone as vain as him, who takes everything for granted. You shrug your shoulders? I'm telling you the truth. Dorian Gray is just good looks. And I am just brains, or art, or whatever you are. And you are just wealth and rank, Helen. We shall all suffer terribly for what the gods have given us—suffer terribly."

Rosemary was surprised by her own frankness—however boldly she sought to live her life, she always tread lightly when it came to the possibility of harming someone's feelings. But Helen only narrowed her icy gaze.

"Dorian Gray? Is that his name?" she asked, walking across the studio toward Rosemary, who got up and paced around the painting.

"Yes, that is his name. I didn't intend to tell you."

"But why not?"

"Oh, I can't explain," said Rosemary with a sigh. "Let's just say I have grown to love secrecy. It seems to be the one thing that can make modern life mysterious or marvelous to us all. Somehow it brings a great deal of romance to life. It brings me pleasure, keeping him a secret. I suppose you think me awfully foolish about it?"

"Not at all," answered Helen. "You seem to forget that I am married, and the one charm of marriage is that it makes a life of deception absolutely necessary for both parties. I never know where my husband is, and he never knows where I am. When we do meet to dine, we tell each other the most absurd stories with the most serious faces. He's not very good at it—I'm much better. I never get confused over the dates like he does. But better I never make a fuss. Best not to have a row."

"I hate the way you talk about your married life, Helen," said Rosemary, strolling toward the door that opened onto the garden. "I believe that you are really a very good wife, but that you are ashamed of your own virtues. You're an extraordinary woman, Helen. You never say a moral thing and never do a wrong thing. Your cynicism is simply a pose."

"Being natural is simply a pose, and the most irritating pose I know," cried Helen, laughing. And arm in arm, the two young women went out into the garden together and ensconced themselves on a long bamboo seat that stood in the shade of a tall laurel bush. The sunlight slipped over the polished leaves. In the grass, the white daisies were tremulous. Rosemary closed her eyes for a moment, luxuriating in the generous sunlight. She'd spent the past four summers here and was always grateful for the garden; a stroll within invigorated her in the morning and quieted her racing thoughts at the end of a long day at the canvas. She let go of Helen's arm and hugged herself, taking a deep, gracious breath inward. She was so tired she could fall asleep just like this. But just as she let herself relax, the image of Dorian Gray burst into her mind, his dark eyes ready to devour her. She gasped and opened her eyes.

"Are you all right?" asked Helen, who was fumbling with her pocket watch.

"Yes, sorry, I've just got so much on my mind. I so appreciate your company, but I'm afraid I'm just not myself lately."

"I wonder why that is," said Helen, smirking.

"Just not getting out enough, I suppose," said Rosemary, wishing Helen could just be a supportive friend for a moment and not such a dubious critic.

"I'm afraid I must be going," said Helen, as if to say such a friend she could not be. "But before I go, I insist you answer my question."

"What is that?" asked Rosemary, eyes fixed safely on the ground. There was no Dorian Gray there.

"You know quite well," said Helen.

"Helen, I really do not," Rosemary said.

"I want you to tell me why you will not exhibit Dorian Gray's picture. I want the real reason."

"I told you the real reason."

"No, you did not. You told me it was because there was too much of yourself in it. Now that is childish.

Why won't you admit that you're in love, and that since you can't have Dorian Gray himself, you will have the next best thing—the splendid painting—where he will forever be in his prime years?"

Helen's words caused Rosemary's heart to quicken. Was it true? She'd not really investigated why she was so unwilling to part with the painting. But now she understood that Helen was right—or halfway right. The situation was more complex. It was not simply that she wouldn't let go of Dorian Gray—though the thought was fearsome—it was that Dorian Gray wouldn't let go of her. Whether he'd meant to or not—and she rather thought he'd meant to— he'd slipped into her subconscious and unlocked a secret attic door, and only he had the key.

The wind shook some blossoms from the trees, and the heavy lilac blooms with their clustering stars moved to and fro in the languid air. A grasshopper began to chirrup by the wall and, like a blue thread, a long, thin dragonfly floated past on its brown gauze wings.

"Let me see you out," offered Rosemary.

"Before I go, will you at least tell me how you met this Dorian Gray?"

"You are such a pain," said Rosemary, feigning annoyance before acquiescing with concealed pleasure. She'd re-created the first moment she saw Dorian Gray dozens of times. It was a thrill to finally share the story with someone, and she could not help but feel giddy.

"Two months ago, I went to a party at Lady Brandon's. Of course, she had prospective suitors she wanted to introduce me to—all of them as dull as the last bunch she picked. Well, I had been in the room about ten minutes, already desperate for escape from the tedious academicians surrounding me, when I became conscious that someone was looking at me. I turned halfway around and saw Dorian Gray for the first time. When our eyes met, I felt I was growing pale. A curious sensation of terror came over me. I knew that I had come face to face with someone whose mere personality was so fascinating that, had I allowed it, it would absorb my whole nature, my whole soul, my very art itself. I did not want any external influence in my life. You know, Helen, how independent I am by nature. I have always been my own master, had at least always been so, till I met Dorian Gray. Then—but I don't know how to explain it to you. Something seemed to tell me that I was on the verge of a terrible crisis in my life. I had a strange feeling that Fate had in store for me exquisite joys and exquisite sorrows. I grew afraid, and turned to quit the room. It was not coincidence that made me do so; it was a sort of cowardice. I take no credit myself for trying to escape."

"Conscience and cowardice are really the same things, Rosemary. Conscience is the trade name of the firm. That is all."

"I don't believe that, Helen, and I don't believe you do either. However, whatever my motive—and it may have been pride, for I used to be very proud—I certainly struggled to the door. There, of course, I stumbled against Lady Brandon.

'You are going to run away so soon, Miss Hall?' she screamed out. You know her curiously shrill voice?"

"Yes. She is a peacock in everything but beauty," said Helen.

"I could not get rid of her. She brought me into the circle of dreadful young men she was positive contained my future husband—and you know I'd really rather die than end up a wife to any of those bores. She spoke of me as her dearest friend. I had only met her once before, but she took it into her head to act as matchmaker. I was writhing to get out when I found myself face-to-face with Dorian Gray. We were quite close, almost touching. Our eyes met again. It was reckless of me, but I asked Lady Brandon to introduce me to him. Perhaps it was not so reckless, after all. It was simply inevitable. We would have spoken to each other without any introduction. I am sure of that. Dorian told me so afterward. He, too, felt that we were destined to know each other."

Helen nodded with interest—these were clearly the details she'd been waiting for Rosemary to divulge. "And how did Lady Brandon introduce this wonderful young man?"

"Oh, she bumbled something like, 'Charming boy—poor dear mother and I absolutely inseparable. Quite forgot what he does—afraid he doesn't do anything—or, yes, plays the piano—or is it the violin, dear Mr. Gray?' Neither of us could help laughing, and we became friends at once."

"Laughter is not at all a bad beginning for a romance, and it is by far the best ending for one," said Helen, who now seemed content to pass the rest of the day in the garden, gabbing about Dorian Gray. The same could be said for Rosemary, but she worried that as she had with the painting, she was putting too much of herself into this conversation. No subject, no matter how provocative, ever transcended idle chatter for Helen, and while she was evidently fascinated by Rosemary's new friend, they could just as easily be talking about actors in a play. For Rosemary, there was much more at stake. To talk of him only magnified his importance to her, and that was a dangerous undertaking.

"I wish you'd stop referring to it as a romance," said Rosemary, who was now tired of sitting in the sun and said so. She declared that they go back into the studio, stood up before Helen could voice her opinion, and went inside.

"Are you upset with me?" asked Helen, as she joined Rosemary on the divan.

"No, I'm just tired," said Rosemary. "I haven't been sleeping well."

"You do know that I consider you like a sister, Rosemary—one I can tolerate unlike my true sisters. You can always talk to me about what's distressing you."

"I see Dorian every day," began Rosemary.

"Well, it is an especially giant canvas," said Helen, elbowing Rosemary's thigh in jocularity. "I'm enveloped in its great shade!"

"No," said Rosemary with a laugh. "I mean I see him daily in the flesh. He sits for me every afternoon—has been for months."

"That seems appropriate," said Helen "You must immerse yourself in the work and not let a day go by."

"Yes, but it's more than that. He makes me happy, Helen. I'm not happy until I see him, and I'm in agony as soon as he leaves. Even now, knowing I will see him soon, my heart is racing with suspense. I need him. I can't live without him."

"How extraordinary!" said Helen, embracing Rosemary as if to congratulate her. "I thought you would never care for anything but your art."

"He is all my art to me now," said Rosemary, her eyes welling. "What oil painting was to the Venetians, the face of Antinous to late-Greek sculpture—that is what Dorian Gray is to me. It is not merely that I paint from him, draw from him, sketch from him. He's my inspiration. You remember that landscape of mine, for which I was offered such a huge price but which I would not part with? It is one of the best things I have ever done because Dorian was sitting beside me while I painted it, just watching me with those mysterious eyes of his. For the first time in my life, I saw in the plain woodland the wonder I had always looked for and always missed."

Helen clapped in excitement. "Extraordinary! I must see this man! How old is he? He looks very young."

"He's actually two years younger than me!"

"And, I assume, unspoken for?"

Rosemary blushed. "We don't talk about such things."

"Oh, innocent little sister," said Helen, coiling a strand of Rosemary's chestnut hair around her finger. "And you're so beautiful. Tell me, is he very fond of you?"

Rosemary squirmed, the all too familiar sensation of desire coursing through her. She crossed and uncrossed her legs.

"He likes me," she said after a pause in which she fought down the swarm of butterflies in her stomach. "I know he likes me. But he seems to take a real delight in giving me pain. The things he says sometimes. He's got . . ." and she paused again, the butterflies in her stomach now fluttering out of fear. She sought the right words, ones that wouldn't provoke Helen. If she told the truth, even jaded Helen would reel with shock. "He just has a very different approach to the world than me."

To Rosemary's relief, Helen didn't inquire further. "You're under the spell of his beauty, certainly. And your art will last longer than his beauty. You will probably tire of him before he tires of you. It's summer now, the days are apt to linger. But soon it will be fall and then winter and the infatuation will die out."

"Helen, don't talk like that," scolded Rosemary. "As long as I live, Dorian Gray will dominate me. You can't feel what I feel. You change too often."

"Ah, Rosemary," said Helen, lighting yet another cigarette. "That is exactly why I can feel it. Those who are faithful know only the trivial side of love; it is the faithless who know love's tragedies."

They sat quietly, with Helen smoking in her self-satisfied way, when suddenly she grabbed Rosemary's arm, her eyes huge with revelation.

"I just remembered!" she cried. "I've heard the name Dorian Gray before!"

Rosemary's heart stammered and plunged. "What? Where?"

"At my aunt's house. She told me she had discovered a wonderful young man who was going to help her in East End, and that his name was Dorian Gray. She didn't mention how good-looking he was—though she did mention that he was earnest and had a beautiful nature. I at once pictured to myself a creature with spectacles and lank hair, horribly freckled, and tramping about on huge feet. I wish I had known it was him!"

Rosemary was nervous thinking of Dorian out on the town. There she was being foolish again. What did it matter to her what he did or who he was with? She couldn't be with him at all times—one could even say she shouldn't be with him in the first place.

"Why ever are you so pale, Rosemary? You look like you may faint."

"I don't want to talk about Dorian Gray anymore," snapped Rosemary. "And I don't want you to meet him and dissect him and inject your poison into his veins."

Just then, the butler tapped on the door, clearing his throat as he readied his announcement.

"Yes, Parker?" said Rosemary.

"Pardon me, Miss," he said, glancing hesitantly at Helen, who smiled curtly in response.

"Dorian Gray is in the sitting room, Miss," said Parker.

If Rosemary was pale before, she was white as a sheet now. Helen jumped up, grabbing Rosemary's hand.

"You must introduce me now!"

Rosemary ignored Helen and looked at Parker. "Please tell Mr. Gray I will be with him in a few minutes," she said. Parker bowed and went up the walk.

"Rosemary!" Helen shrieked.

Rosemary leaped up and grabbed Helen by the shoulders, looking straight at her.

"Please don't seduce him!" she begged. "Don't take away the one person who gives to my art the charm it possesses. My life as an artist depends on him. I'm trusting you, Helen."

"What nonsense you talk!" cried Helen, smiling mischievously and, taking Rosemary by the arm, leading her down the hall toward the sitting room.

CHAPTER II

Rosemary could hear her heart pounding in the throes of anticipation. He was *here*. Every day for weeks she'd had the pleasure, pained though it could be, of seeing *him*—this ecstatic creature who so beguiled and bewitched her. The thrill never dulled. As soon as Parker announced the arrival of Mr. Gray, Rosemary's hands tingled, her breath became a heated pant, and the slow walk down the hall behind the rickety butler became like a walk upon a teetering bridge, every step leaden with anticipation. She could not get to the end of it quickly enough. When she finally reached the door to the sitting room, she was famished for the sight of him.

Helen was determined to be literally one step ahead of Rosemary. Her broad hips were in full, seductive swing, satin skirts thrashing against her surprisingly elegant ankles. She wore the smuggest expression, and her eyes were ablaze with an unfathomable confidence. Rosemary wondered, digging her teeth into her lower lip, how Dorian would respond to a woman so strong and entitled.

He was seated at the piano with his back to them, turning over the pages to a volume of Schumann's "Forest

Scenes." Seeing him at last, Rosemary's heart fluttered with such fury she felt in danger of fainting. *That would make for quite a scene,* she thought. Perhaps he would leap up to catch her and carry her away to bed where he'd restore her with a passionate kiss. She forgot all about Helen. There was no one in the world but Dorian Gray, and here he was, just feet away.

When he turned around, he appeared surprised by Helen. He raised a brow inquisitively at Rosemary. *Just one of our many private communications,* she thought. Not even the devilishly observant Helen would catch the secret exchange of their expressions, their dancing eyes. Rosemary went in for a curtsey that, with her trembling knees, was a near-disaster. Helen arched and dipped like a pro, raising her bundle of fine skirts a little too high above the ankle for Rosemary's taste. She winced as she noticed a faint blush color Dorian's cheeks. He stood to greet them.

"This is Lady Henry Wotton, Helen. She is a dear friend of mine. I have just been telling her what a wonderful sitter you are," said Rosemary, and, feeling her face heat up as she went in for a joke, she said, "And now you stand and spoil your fine reputation!"

Nobody laughed. Helen made a sad, faint *hmph.*

"You have not spoiled my pleasure in meeting you, Mr. Gray," said Helen, stepping forward and extending her hand. "My aunt has often spoken to me about you. You are one of her favorites, and, I am afraid, one of her victims also."

Dorian looked as if his eyes could pop out of his skull. It was likely he had never heard a woman speak so boldly before—and surely not one as peculiarly beautiful as Helen. He regained his repose, and then appeared the wickedly playful smile Rosemary had so anticipated.

"I am in your Aunt Agatha's black books at present," said Dorian, with a funny look of penitence. Rosemary wondered with a quick, needling pain in her breast what such a look meant. Dorian went on. "I promised to go to play a piano duet with her in a show last Tuesday, and I really forgot all about it. This isn't the first time I've been so negligent. I am far too frightened to call."

Helen tilted her head back in a laugh. Rosemary marveled at her. She was so expert in her movements. If Rosemary were to laugh like that, she would probably make a foul snorting sound.

Helen continued. "Oh, I will make your peace with my aunt. She is quite devoted to you. And I don't think it matters about your not showing. The audience probably thought it was a duet. When Aunt Agatha sits down to the piano, she makes quite enough noise for two people."

"That is very horrid to her, and not very nice to me," answered Dorian, laughing. Rosemary beamed with pride. He was a fair match to Helen's wits, to say the least. And what a beautiful laugh he had!

Rosemary read in Helen's eyes as they gazed at Dorian that she was not only finding amusement in Gray's bold wit, but was also rushing to take in his beauty. He was just wonderfully handsome, with his finely curved scarlet lips, his deep gray eyes, his silky gold hair. All the candor of youth was there in him, as well as all of youth's passionate purity. There was something in his face that made one want to get to know him at once, and to be seen by him. Rosemary felt it so strongly. If he wouldn't hold her, he would behold her: She would exist so much more vividly if it was before his eyes.

"Shall we head to the studio?" asked Rosemary, feeling her role reduced to merely that of a painter now that the gorgeous and scene-stealing Helen was present.

"Oh, I am tired of sitting," said Dorian.

Rosemary frowned. "I'm nearly finished," she said.

Dorian shrugged and turned away like a spoiled child. He really could be incorrigible, Rosemary noted with some reassuring sense of disapproval. *Good*, she thought. *I must remember his negative qualities and how unpleasant he can be.*

She rose to lead the way through the hall to the studio. Helen barged in front of her, summoning Dorian's arm, which she grabbed with manhandling brute. Rosemary reminded herself to not take it personally, as Helen insisted on being the center of attention no matter who the audience. But Dorian Gray was hers. No, he was not hers in the way Helen was infamous for having men, but he was as much hers as she'd ever dreamed anyone could be. She could be happy within their limitations.

Back in the studio, Helen flung herself into a large wicker armchair, restlessly folding and unfolding her legs—probably to sneak Dorian a glimpse of her upscale undergarments. Her beauty was strange . . . almost masculine. She was strikingly tall and broad-shouldered, with an imposing posture Rosemary had never known in a woman. She stained her lips a satiny red and wore a peachy rouge on her cheeks, which were always shielded in a diaphanous powder. Her hair was a dark blonde; it was thick and unruly and she never wore it down, keeping it always back in a taut bun. Frizzy tendrils stuck out of the sides, easily engaged with a room's static electricity. Lady Henry Wotton could certainly afford new shoes—boxes of them—but she wore the same dirt-caked Adelaide boots she'd donned for years.

"You are too charming to go in for philanthropy, Mr. Gray—far too charming," Helen was going on in her throaty know-it-all drawl. She opened her cigarette case and offered Dorian a smoke. He politely declined. Rosemary smiled at him.

"And Rosemary, of course, would never smoke," Helen added. "So many things she would never do." It was a pointless jab. Rosemary pretended not to be bothered, tending diligently to mixing colors and preparing brushes. But if Helen kept this up, it would be impossible to work. Was she planning on staying all day? Did she not recognize how precious these final moments with Dorian were? Rosemary imagined Dorian hearing her thoughts and spanking her promptly on her trembling wrist. Of *course* Helen didn't recognize such a thing. No one but Rosemary knew how treasured her times were with Dorian. She had to put up a fight of some kind. She hesitated for a moment and then said firmly to Helen, "Dorian and I agreed to complete our sessions today, and I'm afraid your effortless charms are very distracting."

Helen cocked her head like an exotic parrot who can't fathom what words it is being asked to repeat. *Unbelievable!* Rosemary looked at Dorian for guidance, but he was looking at Helen with sustained intrigue.

"Helen," Rosemary continued, opting for a bolder position. "Would you think it awfully rude of me if I asked you to go away?"

Now it was Helen's eyes that looked about to pop out. Rosemary had never spoken so bravely.

"I'm very sorry," started Rosemary, but Helen shushed her with a disregarding wave. Sucking languidly from her cigarette, she nodded once at Rosemary, then addressed Dorian.

"Am I to go, Mr. Gray?" she asked.

Dorian glanced hopefully at Rosemary, as if she was his mother and Helen a new friend with whom he could meddle in grown-up affairs. What to make of their dynamic?

"It's whatever you wish, Dorian," Rosemary said, frowning.

"Please don't go, Helen," said Dorian. Rosemary had never heard him so earnest. Was he already in love with Helen? Rosemary had an urge to warn him that Helen would eat him alive, would suck him down like one of her drugged cigarettes.

"I want you to tell me why I should not go into philanthropy," Dorian said to Helen.

"I don't know that I shall tell you that, Mr. Gray," started Helen. "It is so tedious a subject that one would have to talk seriously about it. But I certainly shall not run away, now that you have asked me to stop. You don't really mind, Rosemary, do you?" Helen shot a poisonous dart of a look at Rosemary. "You have often told me that you like your sitters to have someone to chat to," she said.

Rosemary bit her lip—she did so whenever she was flustered, which was so often now that Dorian was in her life. She felt Dorian's cold gaze upon her as she bit, and so she held her teeth for just a moment, so the blood flushed to the surface. It was well known between them that this innocent habit of hers maddened him. Ah, it was not so innocent anymore!

"If Dorian wishes it, of course you must stay," said Rosemary, gaining confidence now that she had Dorian's eyes on her. "And, of course, so long as your husband does not mind waiting."

Helen was quick to retort, replying dryly. "We had a very long engagement."

Dorian chuckled. Rosemary gagged. She had never made Dorian laugh with a witty remark—only when she tripped on a stray piece of cord or committed some other act of clumsiness.

He stepped up on the dais with the air of a young Greek martyr. He abhorred having to stay still for so long.

"Rosemary has told me much about you," he said to Helen, speaking like a ventriloquist, his lips hardly moving. "Are you as terrible an influence as she says?"

"Splendid!" Rosemary complimented Dorian on his pose. It wasn't perfect—in fact, it was a bit sloppy, but she was compelled to get back into a zone of one-on-one conversation and put up a window that Helen could only press her nose against. Her jealousy radiated outward like a merciless sun. She began to paint with fevered urgency. Only a few touch-ups to make, she thought, then I'm done with him—with this entire obsession—forever! A second, cruel voice within her chimed in: *And then what will life consist of? Who are you, Rosemary Hall, without Dorian Gray?* Rosemary swallowed both voices and persisted with her work.

Ever delighted by her notoriety, Helen was reveling in the fact that Rosemary had alluded to her as a dangerous woman. "People are so afraid of themselves, nowadays," she carried on. "They have forgotten the highest of all duties, the duty that one owes to one's self. Of course, they are charitable. They feed the hungry and clothe the beggar. But their own souls starve and are naked."

Rosemary blushed at the word "naked" and felt Dorian's eyes on her. There they were, gray as wolves and just as predatory. The heat that had been jealousy gave way to a throbbing desire. How he seized the opportunity to make her squirm. It was as difficult to look him in the eyes as it was to resist them. The heat in Rosemary rose to a stifling degree as Dorian smiled suggestively at her, then ran his eyes down her bodice, following the swell of her breasts. Rosemary's nipples grew erect as his gaze held, then lowered down her corseted waist, then below . . . searching sinfully in the folds of her petticoats. Helen went on talking, but Rosemary was no longer listening and, it seemed, neither was Dorian. Last night's dream played in Rosemary's mind. Instead of fearing the crude acts, Rosemary wanted to re-enact them. Now. With him. Of course, she could not, she would not. This was not the kind of situation for which she'd been saving her maidenhead.

"The finishing touches are nearly complete," she said, breaking the spell between herself and Dorian. "Dorian, could you turn your head a little more to the right?"

Dorian obliged. The repositioning resulted in him looking again at Helen, a perplexingly comfortable misfortune for Rosemary, for the less her eyes had to do with his, the better off she was.

"The only way to get rid of a temptation is to yield to it," said Helen. "Resist it and your soul grows sick with longing for the things it has forbidden itself, with desire for what its monstrous laws have made monstrous and unlawful. You, Mr. Gray, with your rose-red youth and your rose-white boyhood, you have had passions that have made you afraid, thoughts that have filled you with terror, daydreams and sleeping dreams whose mere memory might stain your cheek with shame."

Although Helen's words were directed at Dorian, they rang with terrifying truth in Rosemary's mind.

"Helen, stop trying to scare my guest," she said, trying for a carefree laugh. It sounded like a noise in a zoo.

"The only person scared in this room right now is you, Rosemary," Helen said coldly.

Dorian laughed. *Oh, dear*, thought Rosemary. *Was Dorian really going to team up with Helen now in ridiculing her?* Her heart sank.

The only thing to do, she resolved, was to continue painting as if people were of no consequence to her. Work, she knew, would always save her from the heartache humans could bring; that was why she had fought so hard for this solitary life of art. Her father, widowed and childless save for his bright, beautiful, stubborn daughter, had pleaded with her to reconsider. Never had Rosemary considered any of the young men her father had brought her way. She was rude to them outright, for they stood in her way, tripped up her path like so many pebbles.

She painted away and away, while Helen and Dorian conversed on and on.

"You don't frighten me," said Dorian to Helen, "but you do bewilder me. I don't know what to say. There is some answer to you, but I cannot find it. Don't speak. Let me think. Or, rather, let me try not to think."

Helen, in appreciation of the beguiling effect she had on Dorian, was quiet for a moment, letting him stew in the juices of her sinister logic. She knew the precise psychological moment when to say nothing. *Was she really so evil?* wondered Rosemary. As her friend, she was obliged to think not. Moreover, she felt sorry for her.

Though she only alluded to it in dry self-deprecation, Rosemary knew it to be fact that Helen was barren. Being that she was nearing thirty now, and had given her husband no children in their twelve years of marriage, Rosemary deduced that Helen relied on cruelty as a manner of defense. Where God had denied her womanly softness, she had grown hard. And it was no secret that her husband was wildly unfaithful and frequented brothels without shame.

Rosemary carried on with her painting, but Dorian's posture was caving ever so slightly. Helen's words were coaxing him.

"Rosemary, I am tired of standing," he said. "I must go out and sit in the garden."

"My dear Dorian, I am so sorry. When I am painting, I can't think of anything else," said Rosemary. *Only since meeting him was that statement untrue*, she thought. "You never sat better," she said, though her affect was bland. Really she was just complimenting him to avoid the distress of Helen. "You were perfectly still. And I have caught the effect I wanted—the half-parted lips and the bright look in the eyes. I suppose whatever compliments Helen has been paying you have been effective. But you mustn't believe a word she says."

"She has certainly not been paying me compliments," Dorian asserted. "Perhaps that is the reason that I don't believe anything she has told me."

Rosemary laughed—too loudly—such racket the relief in her heart in seeing Dorian doubt Helen. But Helen was not going to let the mood stay in Rosemary's favor. She looked up with dreamy, languorous eyes.

"I will go out into the garden with you," she offered. "It is horribly hot in the studio. Rosemary, why don't you fix us something iced to drink? Something with strawberries in it?"

Rosemary was infuriated. *Calm*, she told herself. *You must not show her how she gets to you. That will only empower her.*

"Certainly, Helen. Just touch the bell, and when Parker comes I will tell him what you want. I have got to work on this background, so I will join you later on. Don't keep Dorian too long. I have never been in better form for painting than I am today. This is going to be my masterpiece. It is my masterpiece as it stands."

Dorian stretched to loosen his limbs—he loathed keeping still for so long. When he arched his back, there was emphasis on his lean, strapping chest. The muscles of his abdomen rippled under his thin white shirt. Rosemary watched with that funny feeling creeping between her thighs, whetting a mysterious appetite. Some hidden nerve shook in her nether regions. The lips there trembled and longed for a real kiss.

Helen watched Dorian with cunning approval, then got up and strode out into the garden, brushing against his shoulder. Dorian did not so much as glance at Rosemary as he turned around and followed Helen out. Like a puppy whose toy has been taken, Rosemary began to follow them, not sure who at this point—Dorian or Helen—was her master.

The screen door slammed in her face, as the two, by now chummy comrades, continued into the garden, laughing at Helen's private joke.

"I suppose I can work on the background," Rosemary muttered.

CHAPTER III

Though the afternoon was winding down and the sun fading behind the horizon, a palpable heat stirred in the air. Helen sat high on the wicker bench, seeming without a care in the world, but beneath the heap of frilled skirts, her legs lounged open. Sweat trickled down her thighs, and the heat was palpable between them. She ached to be touched and pumped her thighs discreetly, maneuvering the hot, still air.

Dorian seemed to sense Helen's erotic sampling of the weather. He started and drew back. Helen caught a look of fear in his eyes, such as people have when they are awakened. She clasped her hands over her petticoats, against her crotch, allowing some pressure—there had been such a need for attention since she had laid eyes on him. A luxurious sigh escaped her lips as her hooked thumbs fitted against her clenched center. Her inviting gesture and the subdued animal sound that accompanied it caused Dorian to fidget and fumble for a distraction. He buried his nose in the bushel of lilacs neighboring his elbows, feverishly drinking in their perfume as if it were wine.

Helen placed her hand on his shoulder and began to massage.

"You are quite right to do that," she murmured, nodding at the flowers. "Nothing can cure the soul but the senses, just as nothing can cure the senses but the soul."

"Is that right?" asked Dorian.

"Yes," asserted Helen, rubbing her knees discreetly in the piles of her skirts as if to sharpen a point between them. "You are a wonderful creation. You know more than you think you know, just as you know less than you want to know."

Dorian Gray blushed and turned his head away. Helen knew he liked her—that much couldn't be helped—but to what extent he would allow himself was not yet clear. Overripe as she may be at twenty-eight years old, she was still a graceful, beautiful woman with an exquisite figure, unmarred by child labor or any other labor. She had a romantic olive-colored complexion that forbade sunburn and rosy shame in the cheeks. Her eyes were a mystic concoction of light and dark autumnal shades. The color that shone most prominently was a dazzling emerald. Gentlemen and ladies alike readily complimented her eyes, but only the gentlemen complimented her best feature not by speaking but by staring, mesmerized. Her lips were full and perfectly even, with a particularly deep divot in the upper lip. Best of all, they were well-coached in the sport of pleasuring.

Why shouldn't Dorian be seduced by her? To think of all the fun he had probably been depriving himself of thus far! Seducing him would be as simple as unbuckling his belt. Of course there was the matter of getting him to relax and trust her. He was rather like Rosemary, Helen thought, although unlike Rosemary, he surely had some sexual experience and, with proper instruction, would have much more before succumbing to a humdrum marriage.

Helen leaned back into the bench, her hands interlocked on her lap. Dorian braved a glance down at her hands. Helen pushed her thumbs down and groaned so quietly she could have been sighing—that was the trick with these young men: Don't give them too much. Make them wonder if it's their imaginations at work.

The sound of the screen door crashing caused both Dorian and Helen to gasp, as if they'd been caught in the act. It was Parker with their drinks. He set the tray on a matching wicker table in the shade. He gave a bowing nod in Dorian and Helen's direction and left.

Dorian—now jittery—bounced up to get the drinks, but Helen held him back.

"Allow me, darling," she said, and held his shoulder for an extended moment. He was sitting in direct sunlight, she noticed then, and so admonished him. "You really must not allow yourself to become sunburnt. It would be unbecoming."

In the short time it took to collect and deliver the drinks, Dorian was worked up again. The painting had put quite a strain on him.

"What can a sunburn matter?" he cried, with a nervous laugh. He did, however, move into the shade.

"It should matter everything to you, Mr. Gray."

"Why?"

"Because you have the most marvelous youth, and youth is the one thing worth having."

"I don't feel that, Helen."

"No, you don't feel it now. Someday, when you are old and wrinkled and ugly, when thought has seared your forehead with its lines, and repressed passions branded your lips with its hideous fires, you will feel it, you will feel it terribly." Helen duly shuddered. "Now, wherever you go, you charm the world. Will it always be so? . . . You have a wonderfully beautiful face, Mr. Gray."

Dorian folded his hands under his chin and frowned deeply in consideration of Helen's words.

"Don't frown," said Helen. "Beauty is a form of Genius—is higher, indeed, than Genius, as it needs no explanation. It is of the great facts of the world, like sunlight, or springtime, or the reflection in dark waters of that silver shell we call the moon. It cannot be questioned. It has its divine right of sovereignty. It makes princes of those who have it."

She'd restored his good humor and he smiled boyishly. Helen couldn't resist a sincere smile in response. She longed to hold his head and draw him to her for a clandestine kiss. Too soon, she thought, and went on with her speech, veering into even darker subject matter. To incite fear, she'd learned, was a principal maneuver in a first seduction.

"You smile? Ah! When you have lost your good looks, you will not smile. People sometimes say that Beauty is only superficial. That may be so. But at least it is not as superficial as Thought is—nor so destructive. Speaking as a woman on the verge of her own beauty's sun setting, I understand just how superior Beauty is. All that I have is, with each passing moment, becoming all that I had. Soon I will be a worn-out husk that not even my petrified husband will tend to—though that is quite another matter. My point, dear Dorian, is that the Gods have been good to you. But what the Gods give, they quickly take away. You have only a few years in which to live really, perfectly, and fully. When your youth goes, your beauty will go with it. And with your beauty will go your sensual power."

Dorian, spellbound by Helen's words, flinched at this last bit. He looked at Helen for more information. She smiled inside. He was her student now.

"Oh, Dorian, don't be daft. We both know that you have Rosemary, that precious lamb, so willfully naïve to her sexual nature, bordering on hysteria, so captivated is she by this confusing lust. I, too, feel the gravity of your sexual pull, but it does not confuse me. It intrigues me."

Dorian opened his mouth to speak, but Helen pressed a finger against his lips and kept it there. Looking deep into his lively gray eyes, she spoke in a low voice.

"Time is jealous of you, and wars against your lilies and your roses. You will become sallow, and hollow-cheeked, and dull-eyed. You will suffer horribly. . . . Ah! Realize your youth while you have it. Realize your ferocious virility. Don't squander the gold of your days, listening to the tedious, trying to improve the hopeless failure, or giving away your life to the ignorant, the common, and the vulgar. These are the sickly aims, the false ideals, of our age! Live! Seize and master every desire in your heart! Lord over your sexual powers and hold others hostage to them!"

Dorian listened, open-eyed and wondering, his lips drying under the stilling pressure of Helen's finger. He wanted to lick them, Helen noted, but he was hiding the urge. Helen pressed harder, so that soon he would have to pull her hand away. He would have to do *something*.

She went on. "The moment I met you, I saw that you were quite unconscious of what you really are, of what you really might be: a true seducer. In that first look I was so sure you could dominate any girl you wished, that I felt I must tell you. It would be tragic to waste such power while you're still so young and handsome."

Abruptly she released her finger from his mouth. He took a deep breath and licked his lips in relief. She brought her hand to his shirt and pressed his rigid chest. "All that power," she whispered, and moved her hand lower and lower, hesitating purposefully before placing it on his sex. She rubbed ever so gently until she felt it stiffen and rise. It was startlingly large—though not even at its full capacity. The urge to get him at his hardest was tempting, but Helen opted to contradict herself by dismissing the temptation. She had to keep him wanting.

And then the sound of the screen door slamming again. Dorian flung Helen's hands off him and darted up. Helen laughed at him—he was so ridden with good manners!

This time it was Rosemary who emerged. She had freshened up and newly applied some makeup—though in Helen's opinion, she never applied enough—and fixed her hair. She remained by the door and called out, "Do come in! The light is quite perfect, and you can bring your drinks!" And then went back inside.

They rose and sauntered down the walk together. Butterflies fluttered past them, and in the pear tree at the corner of the garden a lone songbird began to sing. Helen searched Dorian's face for evidence of the lust she'd roused in him, but other than the guilty flush on his cheeks, there was no sign that moments ago he'd been surrendered to her.

"You are glad you have met me, Mr. Gray?" said Helen, looking at him with hypnotic intent.

Dorian took in a ruminative breath. He spoke carefully. "Yes, I am glad now. I wonder, shall I always be glad?"

"Always?" cried Helen, nudging him playfully with her elbow. "That is a dreadful word. It makes me shudder when I hear it. It's funny to hear a man use it—normally I hear it from women. I cherish Rosemary, you know, but, ah, how she spoils the idea of romance by thinking the only one worth having is the one that lasts *forever*, which is a meaningless word. The only difference between a caprice and a lifelong passion is that the caprice lasts a little longer."

At the door to the studio, Dorian paused and held Helen's hand. He gazed at her intently. "In that case," he said, "let our friendship be a caprice." He flushed at his own boldness, then opened the door for her. He followed her in and stepped up on the platform by the easel and resumed his pose.

Helen returned to the wicker armchair, much satisfied by her first day in educating the most divine Dorian Gray. She watched Rosemary at work, conscious of wearing a distant expression that indicated boredom. She was, in fact, quite taken with Rosemary's process and envied the girl's impeccable precision. The sweep and dash of the brush on the canvas made the only sound that broke the stillness, except when, now and then, Rosemary stepped back to look at her work from a distance. In the slanting beams that streamed through the open doorway, the dust danced and was golden. The heavy scent of roses seemed to brood over everything.

After about a quarter of an hour, Rosemary stopped painting, looked for a long time at Dorian Gray, and then for a long time at the picture, biting her lower lip and frowning. "It is quite finished," she said at last, and stooping down, she wrote *R. Hall* in vermilion letters on the bottom left-hand corner of the canvas. Helen had been the one to advise her to use only her first initial, rather than her full name, which, she'd said, reeked of their lesser gender.

Helen rose and examined the picture. It was certainly a wonderful work of art and a wonderful likeness as well. Yes, as usual, Rosemary had displayed a most incredible talent. But, as Helen saw it, there was something even more powerful about this painting. It seemed to sing all of Rosemary's unsung desires.

"My dear Rosemary, I congratulate you most warmly," she said. "It is the finest portrait of modern times. Mr. Gray, come over and look at yourself."

Dorian started as if awakened from a dream. "Is it really finished?" he murmured, stepping down from the platform.

"Quite finished," said Rosemary. "And you have sat splendidly today. I am awfully obliged to you."

"That is entirely due to me," broke in Helen. "Isn't it, Mr. Gray?"

Dorian made no answer, but passed listlessly in front of his picture and turned toward it. When he saw it, he drew back, his cheeks flushed with pleasure. A look of joy came into his eyes, as if he recognized himself for the first time. He stood there, motionless and in wonder.

"Do you like it?" asked Rosemary, looking stung by Dorian's silence. Helen almost felt sorry for her. The poor lass had no idea of what had taken place between her and Dorian in the garden—had never known any kind of erotic happening in any garden, or anywhere, for that matter. Helen suppressed a giggle. If Rosemary was stung now, imagine how she'd look if she were to possess any knowledge of the events that had transpired just moments ago!

Dorian remained speechless, so Helen spoke for him.

"Of course he likes it, Rosemary. Who wouldn't like it? It is one of the greatest things in modern art. I will give you anything you like for it. I must have it."

Rosemary looked down and sighed.

"Oh, come now, love, you can and shall part with it," said Helen.

"Yes, I shall part with it," said Rosemary.

"Good girl!" cheered Helen with mock applause. "Now for the real art in all this painting: the business transaction!"

"Oh, no," said Rosemary, biting her lip in a way that most infuriated Helen because it was such a pose for attention. "I'm not selling it," she said. And before Helen could continue, she said, "Nor am I giving it away to anyone. It's not my property, Helen," she said.

"Whose property is it?"

"Dorian's, of course."

"He is a very lucky fellow."

"How sad it is," murmured Dorian, with his eyes still fixed upon his own portrait. "How sad it is! I shall grow old, and horrible, and dreadful. But this picture will remain always young. It will never be older than this particular day. . . . If it were only the other way! If it were I who was always to be young, and the picture that was to grow old! For that—for that—I would give everything! Yes, there is nothing in the whole world that I would not give! I would give my soul for that!"

"You would hardly care for such an arrangement, Rosemary, would you?" Helen scoffed.

"I should object very strongly, Helen."

"Yes, it would be rather hard lines on your work," said Helen, laughing.

"This is not a joke!" cried Dorian. "Helen is perfectly right. Youth is the only thing worth having. When I find that I am growing old, I shall kill myself."

Rosemary turned pale and grabbed Dorian's hand. "Dorian! Dorian!" she cried. "Don't talk like that! I have never had such a friend as you, and I shall never have such another. You are not jealous of material things, are you? You are finer than any of them!"

"I am jealous of everything whose beauty does not die. I am jealous of the portrait you have painted of me. Why should it keep what I must lose? Every moment that passes takes something away from me, and gives something to it. Why did you paint it, Rosemary? It will mock me some day—mock me horribly!" He tore his hand away from Rosemary, and, flinging himself on the divan, he buried his face in the cushions as if he was praying.

"This is your doing, Helen," said Rosemary bitterly.

Helen shrugged. "It is the real Dorian Gray—that is all."

"It is not."

"If it is not, what have I to do with it?" asked Helen, coyly.

"You should have gone away when I asked you to," muttered Rosemary.

"I stayed when you asked me."

"Helen, I can't quarrel with my two best friends at once, but between you both, you have made me hate the finest piece of work I have ever done, and I will destroy it.

What is it but canvas and color? I will not let it come across our three lives and mar them."

Dorian lifted his head from the pillow and, with pallid face and tear-stained eyes, watched Rosemary move to the desk where she stored her utensils. She opened a drawer and dug around, her fingers straying among the litter of tin tubes and dry brushes. She pulled out a long knife with a thin blade of lithe steel.

With a stifled sob, Dorian leaped from the couch and, rushing over to Rosemary, tore the knife out of her hand, and flung it to the other end of the studio. "Don't, Rosemary," he said, regaining his composure. "That would be murder."

"I'm glad you appreciate my work at last, Dorian," said Rosemary in a hurt tone. "I never thought you would."

"Appreciate it?" said Dorian. "I am in love with it, Rosemary. It is part of myself. I feel that."

"Well, as soon as you are dry, you shall be varnished and framed and sent home," said Rosemary. She wiped her hands on the rag that hung on her easel. "Then you can do what you like with yourself."

Helen, relishing the drama, jumped to her feet and clapped.

"Bravo!" she cried, ecstatically. Dorian smiled sheepishly at Helen, much recovered from the moment's theatrics.

"Helen, please," said Rosemary. "I'm exhausted now. I think it's best that I just retire early. Painting this intensely, for so long, always drains me." She turned to Dorian with a look of sadness in her eyes that perplexed Helen. "I'm sorry, Dorian. I hope you shall soon excuse me to lie down."

"We shall," answered Helen. "We're going to the theater."

"The theater?" said Dorian and Rosemary in unison. Dorian laughed and shook his head as if he couldn't keep up with this Helen Wotton, but thought it was a fun chase. Rosemary looked as if she could retrieve the knife.

"I entreat you," Helen said to him.

Dorian hesitated and looked over at Rosemary, who was watching with a mournful look from beside the canvas.

"I must go with Helen," he said.

"Very well," said Rosemary.

"Thank you," he said, and went to her with his hand extended. With apparent reluctance, she gave him hers. He granted it a quick kiss.

"She won't like you the better for going," said Rosemary suddenly. Then, she urged him in a whisper that was loud enough for Helen to hear: "I beg you not to go."

Dorian only nodded politely. "Get some rest, dear," he said and headed for the door. Helen followed. Just as she was exiting, Rosemary ran to her and grabbed her by the shoulder.

"I trust you," she whispered. Her lovely blue eyes were wild with worry.

Helen wrapped her arms around Rosemary. "I wish I could trust myself," she whispered into Rosemary's ear, then leaned down and gave her a lingering kiss on the lips, nudging her tongue gently to part them what little way they'd go.

CHAPTER IV

Helen's driver, Edgar, was a small man with a weathered, alcoholic complexion and permanently chapped lips. He'd started his work with the Wottons as the driver of Helen's husband, Lord Henry Wotton, but was fired after he drunkenly careened the carriage into a tree with Lord Wotton inside. Lord Wotton had not been alone, and the whore—whose mouth was hard at work in his lap at the time of the accident—was thrown out of the cab and left with a broken jaw and the end of a career.

Helen, feeling that Edgar was of some use (he was, after all, loyal, and did, after all, have a tireless tongue that could fleck her cunt for hours), hired him as her own driver. He was in love with her in that worshipful, self-ruining way that gets people killed long before they muster their last breath. He couldn't bear to look her guests in the eye for he knew that, like her husband, Helen took full advantage of her company in the bouncing carriage.

The beautiful Dorian, with the piercing gray eyes and the strong, tall build, must have been a painful sight for the dwarfish driver. He hurried to settle the two inside, then ran around to reclaim his post on the back of the hansom. The horses lunged forward as Helen shouted instructions.

"Edgar, please take us to Regent Street. To Verrey's," she ordered.

Dorian's eyebrows rose. Verrey's was one of London's more expensive restaurants. And it was miles away.

"Certainly you've been there?" said Helen.

"No," Dorian said quietly. "No, not yet."

"Hmm, curious. You know, I really am dying to know your situation. It's clear from your dress and manner that you're hardly a beggar."

Dorian eyed her suspiciously. "If you already know, why do you ask?"

"To know better," said Helen, stripping off her gloves. She nestled beside Dorian like a loving sister and grasped his hand. His mouth went rigid in a frown. "I'm really quite common in that I always like to hear the bad news first. Dorian, tell me about your mother."

Dorian sighed and looked with deep thought out the window. "She was an extraordinarily beautiful woman," he said at last.

"I imagine her nothing but," said Helen.

"The bluest eyes you've ever seen, I'm told. She could have married anybody she chose, and plenty of rich and handsome men were mad after her. She had a husband here, in England. They had a daughter together, but she died, I'm told. I don't know. I never met the husband or even learned his name. He loved her more than she loved him, though, of that much I am certain. A true romantic, she left him, and fled to America, which is where she met my father—a penniless young fellow, a mere nobody. He was killed in a duel a few months after I was born. It was an ugly story, one that was never fully divulged to me, but I have picked up scraps of details growing up. I believe that her husband—to whom she was still legally bound—got some rascally adventurer, some Belgian brute, to insult my father in public, paid him to do it, and that the fellow did away with my father as if he had been a pigeon. The thing was hushed up, and my mother soon fell ill and died. My Great-Uncle Kelso arranged for me to be brought to London. Ultimately, he did the right thing by me, and when I came of age, I had a pot of my mother's money waiting for me."

So that was the story of Dorian Gray's parentage. Crude as it was, it stirred Helen by its suggestion of a strange, almost modern romance. A beautiful woman risking everything for a mad passion. A few wild weeks of happiness cut short by a hideous, treacherous crime. Months of voiceless agony, and then a child born in pain. The mother snatched away by death, the boy left to solitude, and the tyranny of an old, loveless man. Yes, it was an interesting background. It made him more perfect as it were, because behind every exquisite thing that existed, there was something tragic. Helen was overcome with the urge to possess and dominate him, to make this wonderful spirit, this son of Love and Death her own.

She smiled and clutched Dorian's hand tighter. He looked to her for what to feel next. There was something terribly enthralling in the exercise of influence. No other activity was like it. To convey one's temperament into another as if it were a subtle fluid or a strange perfume—there was a real joy in that.

"Dorian," she started. "Those who find ugly meanings in beautiful things are corrupt without being charming. This is a fault. When you—"

And here Dorian interrupted Helen, leaping up and kissing her on the mouth. His breath was hot, his tongue was searching. She'd never been kissed with such intensity. Usually, men went through such political steps—they sought the right moment, a certain expression in the damsel's eye. They were careful not to be rough, and fumbled for momentum. They saved their real kisses for whores.

While kissing her, he climbed on top of her, his thumbs digging into her shoulders, pinning her beneath him. His strength was impressive, and if he were to really let go, he could go to marvelous lengths. He was still operating with a good deal of self-restraint, Helen sensed, probably due to the smallness of the carriage, and so she refused to allow him to overpower her. She fought back, slamming him into the door. She circled his tongue with hers, their mouths enmeshed, then she bit down on his lip hard. Harder. A whimper escaped him, brief and muffled. He buried his head in her neck, and fixated there, began to suck with ferocity, rubbing her breasts. Helen tossed her head back and moaned.

"Bite me," she commanded.

There was a brief moment of hesitation before he sunk his teeth into her, biting as hard as she'd bit his lip, only he didn't let go, keeping his teeth clamped to her neck, while his hands rushed through the complicated affair of undoing her corset, tearing her loose with the one snatch.

Helen brought her hands to his scalp and tugged his locks of lush blond hair by the roots. Each time she tugged, he kissed her more forcefully, but when she pulled so hard she felt a hair snap, he slapped her hands away and seized her hair by the bun and yanked it loose. She spread her legs apart, and he pushed himself against her, his cock lunging. She ran her hands down his shirt, popping the buttons. She unfastened his belt and pants and, while fondling his massive erection with both hands, slid her knickers down. All the while, the carriage, gaining speed, bobbed and bounced on the uneven cobblestone.

She sunk to the floor of the carriage where the rocking was more intense. She kept a one-handed massaging grip on his heated, throbbing cock while bringing the other hand to her mouth, where she licked it, pooling spit in her palm. She brought the moistened hand back down his cock and glided her fingers loosely around it with ease. Dorian closed his eyes and moaned in ecstasy. She moved her hand faster, jerking the skin around his cock back and forth, and tightened the pressure of her thumb at the base of his cock. The rhythm intensified, his cock quivered and lunged. Seeing that he would explode into her hand at any moment, Helen abruptly let go.

Dorian gasped and opened his eyes. He glared at her with animal hunger, panting.

"What?" he said. "Why did you—?" His good manners stopped him, so he was unable to complete the sentence.

"Why did I stop rubbing your cock?" asked Helen.

Dorian was silent.

"If you're so eager to come like a schoolboy, why don't you finish the business yourself like a schoolboy would?"

He didn't utter a word, and for what felt like the first time since she was a girl, Helen found herself unable to read the expression on the face before her. There was the let-down, of course, as he held a terrific erection in his agile hands. And there was anger—that she'd taken him this far only to abandon him so close to the end. But there was vacuousness, too. His eyes, so many shades of gray, were strangely devoid of feeling. They bore through her, so hollow and with the power to hollow out everything they set sight on. Helen felt her soul emptying, offering itself to him. The sexual ache in her crotch flared, and dripped warmly on the cool leather seat.

As if possessed, she lifted her skirts and leaped onto him. In a hurry, she fit herself onto him. His cock filled her up. So large, it pushed against the walls of her vagina, probing unexplored zones of pleasure. As she began to grind, she felt a delicious sensation—that if he took full advantage and rammed into her as far as he could, he could break some virgin remnant within her. She straddled him tightly with her thighs and moved slowly up and down. Delight swelled inside her. Dorian held her sternly by the thighs, rocking her back and forth. His eyes rolled into his head, and, moved by a bizarre tenderness toward him, this new creature of pure beauty and the ability to give ungainly pleasure, Helen ran her hands through his hair—a quite unwelcome gesture. Dorian slapped her hand away and held her wrist firmly so she couldn't make such a move again.

He moved a hand up her thigh to her ass and squeezed her cheek. Helen felt him raise his hand. In anticipation, she rode him harder, got him in deeper. As she began to climax, he spanked her sharply. In a sexual delirium devoid of self-control, Helen shrieked.

"Yes," she cried. "Spank me, Dorian. Punish me!"

He slapped her again and again, three times, ten times. She lost count. The pleasure was ruthless. Helen arched her back as her calves flexed and tightened. She was nearly going to explode. She ceased to thrust, but Dorian kept up the rhythm, plunging into her repeatedly. She threw her head back and let out a long cry as he smacked her ass relentlessly. There was no controlling it now. When he thrust into her again, she came long and gloriously, rushing his cock with warm secretions.

She continued to ride him, working to get him to come, too. Her thighs radiated with exhaustion. Then he pushed her off him.

"Get down," he ordered.

She got onto the floor of the carriage. She placed her hands on his knees and, without further instruction, took his bulging cock into her mouth. When he held her head, she slapped his hands away. She sucked and rolled her tongue along the head. Dorian's breath quickened.

"Ah!" he cried, his cock twitching against the roof of her mouth.

When she felt he was close, she withdrew him from her mouth, letting just her tongue linger, and grasped his cock with her hand. She gave several rapid jerks, and when he lurched the penultimate lurch, she closed her eyes. His sperm burst hotly all over her face.

Dorian fell back into his seat and caught his breath. Helen gathered her underwear, which her desire had moderately soiled, and slid them back on. She sat back beside Dorian and noted an exquisite smarting in her insides, where his cock had plumbed her so thoroughly. Her bottom rang sorely in the bruised aftermath of his beating.

Dorian quietly repaired his own disarray. He pulled and tucked and buttoned himself back into place. Within minutes, it was as if the whole thing hadn't happened. Ah, but there was the detail of his drying seed on her face.

"Dorian," she said. She bunched up her skirt and held it out to him.

"Yes?" he said, looking at her with confusion.

"Please spit."

Dorian cringed.

"No," said Helen, bringing the skirt closer to his face. "Spit. Now."

Dorian rolled his eyes, but obliged at last.

"Thank you," she said, and with the wet part she wiped her face.

She took out her pocket mirror and applied a sheath of powder to her nose and forehead. The looking glass revealed the clouded eyes and rosy complexion of a woman who'd just been properly fucked. She smiled at herself, and thought of Rosemary biting her lower lip. What the dear thing had coming to her! Helen imagined her nude on the floor of her studio, surrendered in submission, while Dorian ravaged her.

Dorian. What a marvelous find he was! Grace was his, and the white purity of boyhood, and beauty such as a Greek god's. There was nothing that one could not do with him. He could be made a Titan or a toy. What a pity it was that such beauty was destined to fade!

"I believe we are nearly there," said Helen.

Dorian was gazing out the window. A solemnity had draped the carnal mood.

"Something on your mind?" Helen asked. Gentleness did not come easily to her, but she managed to muster a kind voice. Dorian seemed deep in a thought he would never share. At last, he turned to Helen.

"I think I'd like one of those cigarettes, if you don't mind, Lady Wotton."

Helen managed to conceal any reaction to being called by her married title, and withdrew her cigarette case.

"Consistently one of the great ideas of our time," she said. "A smoke."

Just then, the carriage began to slow.

"Ah! We must be here," Helen said. She was eager to get out into the open air with Dorian, and then to cozy up to a bottle of gin. But no—she heard Edgar whip the horse.

"No," she said with a sigh, for the solemnity was infectious. "We actually aren't there yet."

There was a brief whinny from the horse, then the galloping speed resumed.

CHAPTER V

At half past twelve a week later, Rosemary Hall turned in the direction of Berkeley Square to call on her father, Edmund Hall, a genial if somewhat rough-mannered old widower whom the outside world called selfish because it derived no particular benefit from him, but who was considered generous by Society as he fed the people who amused him. He was a retired diplomat, and was now dedicated to pursuing the aristocratic art of doing absolutely nothing. He had two large townhouses, but preferred to live in chambers, as it was less trouble, and took most of his meals at the club. He loathed American influences and was convinced that England was going to the dogs. His principles were out of date, but there was a good deal to be said for his prejudices.

When Rosemary entered the room, she found her father sitting in a rough shooting coat, smoking a pipe, and grumbling over a newspaper.

"Rosemary!" he cried, and stood with outstretched arms.

"Father!" Rosemary ran to him and fell into his bearish embrace.

"What brings you out so early? I thought you artist types never got up until noon and weren't visible until two."

Rosemary laughed and held him tightly. "Father, I just stopped by to show you something. And then I have to go deliver it elsewhere. And I may never see it again!"

She flew out of his grasp and ran to the door where she'd propped the painting. She was behaving erratically, this she knew—talking fast, unable to stay focused, in a frenzied toss-up between laughter and tears. It had been days since she had any sleep, ever since Dorian vanished with Helen. She hadn't heard from either of them.

Last night had been the worst of all, though. Not even the sordid dream had come to whisk her into oblivion. Exhaustion wracked her body, and she felt feverish. She had prayed—reciting not just her nightly prayers but new ones altogether. She prayed to be cleansed of her desire so that she could be returned to a mind of purity. She apologized to God for lusting. Yet a part of her didn't feel sorry. A part of her was lying to her Lord. An horrific thought struck her: *Is Dorian Gray now my Lord?*

No, of course not, she told herself. She was just acting hysterical and needed to calm down. She took a long bath and drank an herbal tea laced with laudanum that Helen had given her. The tea put her in a stupor that reduced her anxieties. The volume of her thoughts decreased. Consciousness lazed in a dull, sprawling babble. But every time she nodded off, the memory of Helen's cackling broke through and the image of Dorian looking at Helen with such intrigue, such inspiration, lightning-bolted through her mind, shedding a cruel light on all her loneliness therein.

Questions swarmed her. What had happened after they left? What was happening at that moment? Were they still together? Was he in love with Helen? Helen always talked about her husband's indiscretions, but Rosemary knew that Helen entertained many of her own. Would she use and discard Dorian the way she did her other lovers? Or would she fall in love with him, too?

By the time dawn seeped in and the chirping of birds livened the trees, Rosemary was still wide awake with dread. She tried to pass the time with painting, returning to an old landscape piece she'd abandoned when she met Dorian. Nothing had ever felt so hideously boring, and in a nervous fit she splattered a half-bucket of red paint on it—the bloodiest shade in her collection. The only painting she'd ever connected with, she was now tragically convinced, was the painting of Dorian. He was her love, her life. Now that Helen had taken him away from her, she could no longer hide from the truth. So she set to framing the painting, using her favorite silver frame that had been a gift from her father. She would then wrap it up and deliver it to Dorian and be done with it and, oh, possibly him, forever.

But she needed her father to see the gorgeous work she created. She needed just another moment in its fantasy, and a final approval.

When she unveiled it for her father, he was visibly moved, his eyes wide with wonder.

"Rosemary, my dear!" he cried. "This is magnificent!"

"Yes, yes, I know. Isn't he? He's so wonderful, father. But I won't see him again. No, I can't. Do you like the way the light is caught in his eyes? Have you ever seen eyes so mysterious? They're gray, but so many shades of gray. Like stone. The way the light does that—it took hours for me to make it right, but that's just how he looks. Oh, father! I'm getting rid of it forever, and I just wanted you to see it before it is gone."

Her father nodded as she spoke, trying to follow her, his furry white eyebrows knitted in confusion. She went on and on until she was breathless, then collapsed into the nearest chair.

"Darling," said her father. He came over to her and put a hand on her shoulder. "You're very fatigued. Why don't you take a nap?"

"I can't sleep," she said, clutching his hand. She peered up at him, her cried-out eyes brimming once again.

"And I hear Georges Petit wants to feature you in a show this fall," said her father. *Oh, yes*, thought Rosemary. *George Petit*. Once that meant something to her.

"This painting of yours will be the crowning glory of the collection!" said her father. He patted her shoulder, then, sensing her pain, tilted her chin up in his palm, his expression radiating the fatherly love she so trusted.

"Such blue eyes," he said, his tone pensive and somewhat forlorn. "Such an angelic face. So much like your mother's when I met her, when she held you in her arms. Oh! I am sorry you couldn't have known her the way I did—though, well, one can't really say I knew her that well."

"Oh, father, it is not at all your fault," said Rosemary, beginning to tear up. She felt deeply for her father. How did one go on after losing their soul mate? Ah, to experience a love like theirs! Even if it must end too soon.

Her father took a deep, restorative breath and blinked away his tears. It was an overwhelming joy to see her father behave so humanly, and Rosemary's suffering seemed to lose all importance. She found renewed purpose in comforting him.

"God took her and made her an angel, father," she said. "He took her when she was too young, yes, but now she will always be young. Who wants to grow old and decay? We do it because we must. But no matter what, her love for you will go on, just as it goes on for me. It is a great tragedy that she had to leave us, but she didn't want to. I feel her presence always. You must feel it, too." She waved a hand toward the garden. "Especially now with the poppies in bloom! Just like her favorite flower, she was beautiful, but short-lived."

Her father drew a strand of chestnut hair from her cheek. The long night's tossing and turning had left her disheveled. Hairpins stuck out of her bun at random, and the bun itself was a mess. She'd been too manic that morning to be bothered with adjusting it.

"Rosemary, my sweet child," said her father, petting her cheek and looking into her eyes. Tears swelled to the brink of his eyelids but did not cross over. "I have waited so long to tell you something."

Rosemary's heart leapt in fear. "Father," she stood to face him closely. "Father, what is it? Your stomach? The bloat?!" she cried, bringing a hand to his sizable belly. "Have your symptoms returned? That look on your face! Father, you must tell me these things at once. No more secrets!"

Defeat shadowed his face, followed by a sad smile.

"No, Rosemary, no more secrets. Please sit down again."

Rosemary hesitated but obeyed and waited. Her frenzy was now past the point of thoughts. She was hanging onto sanity now, clawing at it with her soul, about to slip. . . .

"Tell me," she said.

Her father turned away and began to pace around her. Rosemary clutched her hands, ready for prayer.

"Your mother didn't die when you were a child," he said.

"What?" asked Rosemary. The sanity she was digging into for support quaked with earthly disregard.

"Well," he debated with himself. "Technically, she did die when you were a child. But not in that house. Not in that so-called deathbed you sleep in so that you may feel closer to her spirit. In truth, she quite detested that bed— at least she did in the nighttime, given that I was always in it then."

"Father, what are you saying?!"

"I'm saying your mother left me—she left you, Rosemary—she ran off with a destitute degenerate, an American! She paid his way with her Shelby property. Your Uncle Kelso turned the other cheek." He shook his bald, shining head. "Rosemary, your mother abandoned us."

Rosemary was too stunned to respond immediately. Rage, hurt, resentment, and shame seared through her. And the questions—so many questions—one sprouting off the other, all piling up in her heart like dead leaves, for what was the use in answering them now? The damage was done.

"You lied to me," she said, her voice strange and other-worldly, as though she was her own ghost.

"Rosemary, I only wanted to protect you."

"You lied to me!" Rosemary repeated. She stood up and shouted in her father's face. "You lied to me, lied to me! Every-thing I've ever known was a lie!"

"Please," he begged, beginning to weep. "I love you. Your mother loved you. For a while. I mean, I'm sure she never stopped loving you, she just found someone that she loved more than me. They had a son, Rosemary. You have a half-brother."

"Ah!" Rosemary cried, her hands were balled up in fists at her side. She needed something to hit. Her father would be an ideal target, but she couldn't stand being in the same room with him any longer. She had to get out.

The painting. The painting and Dorian. That was all she had left in this world, and by God, they must save her.

She ran to the painting and sloppily wrapped it back up, then started for an exit. As she was turning the latch, she turned back to look at her father. He had dropped into the chair she'd been seated in, head in his hands. He was weeping softly and muttering incoherently to himself.

Would this be the last time she ever saw him? Right now, she thought—if she had any control over it—yes.

"Take care of yourself, father," she said.

He lifted his head from his hands. His face was red and bulbous, wet with tears and the runny nose that always comes so crudely with the territory.

"I only told you because—that painting, it's so remarkable, Rosemary!" he cried. "You're truly an adult with that work. It's foolish of me to continue covering your eyes from the truth. I respect you too much."

The words she'd so long waited to hear from him went straight through her. Years of yearning for him to believe in her—not just because he was inclined to as her father, but because, as a man of intelligence, he was genuinely impressed—now felt like a waste of time. What did his support matter if he was not honest with her? Financially speaking, it was her mother's money that got her by. She didn't need her father for that. When she left, she shut the door so quietly it was as if it had been closed all along. *Like I was never there*, she thought, *like I never even existed.*

CHAPTER VI

A volatile summer storm was heading for London. The sky was ashen, with low clouds and a rumbling thunder in the distance. Soon it would pour, and Rosemary, having done such a haphazard job of wrapping the painting, was risking it getting water damage. Still, she took her time. A couple of young men offered to help her, for the painting was visibly heavy and Rosemary tipped precariously under its awkward weight, looking like a girl who may faint. She caught her reflection in the painting's shiny frame and scarcely recognized the deathly looking girl with the chalky complexion and the dark half-moons under the eyes.

She'd been to Dorian Gray's home once before, but it was in secret. Not even he had known that she was there. It was early in their friendship, the night she first had the dream, where her subconscious took reign and her body lunged beyond her control. In the dream, Dorian was on top of her, but he had only his shirt off, and her hands grazed the smooth mounds of muscle. She still had her knickers on but his hand was reached down them, playing its way finger by finger down, down, down. His forefinger traced the folds of her vagina and circled around her clitoris for a stretch of time that was Paradise and Hell at once. When he finally touched her there, the climax was immediate and seized every muscle in her body. It was when she was about to explode that she woke up and, dazed, realized she was furiously rubbing herself against the mattress. As soon as she thought to stop herself, she exploded, muffling her hard-earned cry of release into the pillow.

Never before had she known such a dream, and certainly she hadn't ever found herself relating to her bed in such a way. Too shaken to fall back asleep, she waited for dawn, then hailed a hansom and rode to Dorian's house. She emerged from the cab but was intent on not being seen. She lurked outside the gate, touching the gold poppies, feeling that in doing so she might collect some sacred essence of Dorian. Just knowing she was close to him was all she needed. The sky had been pure opal, and the roofs of the houses glistened like silver against it. The peace in knowing he was sleeping just yards away was the greatest she could remember.

This time, she didn't bother with hailing a hansom. That would be too reasonable a choice, and this was a day for spitting in the face of reason. It was a day for walking too far, for carrying too much, for being too alone when the rain began to fall.

Exhausted and beaten down by betrayal (and chances were she would hear of more betrayal regarding her oh-so-dear friend—*really, like a sister*—Helen!), Rosemary couldn't think straight. The facts she'd just learned from her father fled before her mind like frightened forest things. Around them swirled hallucinatory horrors: Helen's chilling laughter, Dorian's gray eyes aglow with intrigue as he listened to Helen's depraved teachings, the toxic smoke floating from Helen's languid exhalations.

It was nearly three o'clock in the afternoon when she arrived at Dorian's home. She did not knock right away, but loitered on the doorstep, looking for signs of life— and finding none in the blank close-shuttered windows and their staring blinds. Clutched by the anxious thought that he could be in bed with Helen, she set the painting down and pounded on the door. An elderly valet opened the door at once as if he'd been waiting for her.

"Yes?" he said, taking in her disheveled appearance with-out a flicker of surprise in his sunken old eyes.

"Ahem," Rosemary became self-conscious and straightened herself as best she could. *Oh my*, she thought. *What am I wearing?* She had an ample collection of dresses, but chose a most ragged one so old and ill-fitting that she used it only when painting. It was flecked with the myriad colors of sunsets and oceans and alabaster moons—and the gray soul of Dorian's eyes.

"Good afternoon, Sir," she said, submitting a bow of her head as she was unable to curtsey with the ungainly painting in her arms. "I am here to see Mr. Gray."

The sunken eyes registered her with a heavy blink.

"Mr. Gray did not say he was expecting anyone," replied the valet.

There was a dagger of lightning and then a slam of thunder that made Rosemary jump.

"Yes, I'm afraid we didn't settle on an exact time," said Rosemary.

The rain began.

The valet looked at the wrapped painting in her hands and then at the growling sky, seemingly unimpressed with both. Rosemary huddled closer to the door for shelter, hoping she could inspire some empathy in the man.

"Please," she said. "May I just step inside for a moment?"

She mustered a chatter of her teeth, though it was quite warm out.

The valet seemed to consider, then at last he backed away from the door, leaving her just enough room to slip in with the painting.

"You may wait here while I see if Mr. Gray is available," he said.

"Thank you," said Rosemary, entering. "I have a painting here for Mr. Gray and I know he would be devastated if it were soaked."

"Yes, you chose a fine day for delivery," he muttered. He took the portrait from her and set it carefully against the wall.

Rosemary found herself in a somewhat somber hall with richly lacquered wood and high ceilings at the back of which was a spiral wainscot staircase. A pelt of wind slammed the door behind her, causing her to jump yet again. A magnificent chandelier made a mild stir above.

Rosemary had long tried to picture what Dorian's home was like, and it came as no surprise that it was large and impeccably maintained. But there was a gloom and imperious silence she'd not anticipated. Something about it felt unlived in, *unloved* in, even. Dorian Gray, the charismatic youth of such astonishing beauty and grace was . . . lonely? Unfathomable! Yet the sense of isolation was present everywhere Rosemary looked. Even the valet, with his eyes like worn, sapless wood, was a kind of loneliness personified.

"You may wait here," said the valet. He grunted and headed up the stairs, looking down on her throughout his ascent.

Rosemary wondered what to do with herself in the huge hall. There was a chill present that she hadn't noticed outside, and she had gotten wet in the sudden downpour. She hugged herself and stood by a bare coat rack, the least valuable looking thing in the room.

It was not long before she heard the slow steps of the valet plodding down the stairs.

"Mr. Gray is having his breakfast in his private dining room," he said, pointing listlessly up the stairs. "To your right," he said. "And then the first door on your left. It is open." He then promptly forgot all about her, disappearing behind a pair of doors leading out to a back patio.

Peculiar. Who had a dining room on the second floor? And who took breakfast so late in the day? It occurred to Rosemary that Dorian may have some quirks to his personality. It was a refreshing idea, and the first time she'd ever considered him to be anything but perfect. Newly inspired, she left the painting where it was and went up the stairs. The only nervousness she felt was that of excitement. She had missed Dorian.

At the landing, the house parted ways with itself and split up into two wings. Rosemary turned right, toward the west wing, where she passed through a door that opened unto a hallway. On her left was a smaller door with a sliver of pale light indicating it was ajar. She tapped lightly just as a bolt of thunder rattled the windows. She pushed the door open.

Dorian sat alone at a small oak table. The room appeared to have been a bedroom that was converted into a dining room, with a terrace attached. Stooped over his plate, Dorian emanated a most unusual dejection. Pangs of adoration and self-consciousness took turns at Rosemary. She cursed herself for coming here and wanted to run away. If only she'd collected herself before rushing over here. She felt Helen's familiar reprimand, *"So dramatic!"* hissing like a snake.

Oddly, Dorian did not turn to see her when she entered, though he seemed aware of her presence, for he stopped eating and sighed as if he had to face something he'd been dreading. Rosemary deemed it best to act exceedingly happy.

"Why, good morning there!" Rosemary said with forced cheer. "Though, actually it is high afternoon. May I?" She gestured to the vacant seat beside him. He nodded and yawned loudly, then returned to his eating. He still would not look at her. She took the seat.

Being close to him still held its humiliating enchantments. She bowed her head shyly, a flush of pleasure stealing into her cheek. Biting her lower lip, she wondered what facile excuse she could invent for her appearance, not to mention her inexplicable frenzy and showing up at his door without invitation. *Act as if nothing is wrong*, she thought. *Just be natural.* But what was natural anymore? She was not the same person that she was before she met Dorian Gray. Ah, she wasn't even the same person she was hours ago! Her father, the only man in her life, the man she worshipped and trusted with the entirety of her being, was just a liar. The celestial angel she'd long to know all her life—her mother—hadn't even loved the pathetic man. Ah, that angel was a fallen one, perhaps.

"Dorian," she started at last. "I'm sorry for not telling you that I'd be coming at this hour, but I figured I was more or less expected, since we agreed that you would take the painting as soon as it was ready to go. I thought it would be done days ago, but since I didn't hear from you, I really didn't think it was much of a rush. But, wouldn't you know, paint takes so long to dry! Much longer than you'd think. It always surprises me—even after all these years!"

Oh, dear. She was so nervous that she was going to just keep talking. Usually, when she did this, Dorian looked at her with amusement, a spark of flirtation lighting up his eyes. But today he was altogether indifferent. He just went about finishing his food, now and again dabbing his chin (which was uncharacteristically stubbly) with a silk napkin that bore his initials in a steel-colored thread. When he was done, he tossed the napkin on the crumb-filled plate and took a long sip of his tea.

Still, he said nothing. It was as if he was stalling or perhaps preparing to make eye contact with Rosemary, who was willing him to look at her. She needed him. She needed him to love her.

"Dorian," she said. At last, his eyes on hers. His face was as beautiful as ever, and there were no signs of fatigue, but there was an absence in his eyes, an unknown darkness filling it. Rosemary went on chatting, but now, with his cold gaze upon her, so stark and unfeeling, she felt that she was on the brink of a wonderful danger.

"You look well," she said, her voice trembling. "Yes, as well as ever! But, honestly, you do seem rather withdrawn and seeing that you've taken your breakfast so late, I'm prompted to ask: Are you feeling all right?"

In the background rose a sudden, small dinging of a bell. It startled Rosemary, and she looked around for the source. Then, glimpsing the service bell on the other side of Dorian, she realized it was him ringing it. In a flash, the old valet swooped in and cleared the table. In another flash, he was gone.

Dorian stretched in his chair and yawned again. He rubbed his eyes as if his head ached. It seemed he'd been going over and over a problem in his mind, sleeplessly, for days. Yet he really did look well. He looked beautiful, in fact. She was not surprised when he did not say the same of her.

"You look thin," he said, speaking at last—his voice hoarse and dry as if these were the first words he'd spoken since waking. "I hate when you become thin," he said, looking at her with black eyes. Rosemary had never seen them so lightless. And his tone was so begrudging. How at odds his unblemished face was with his manner! He was like a water lily: What one saw of him was the bright, vivacious beauty bobbing on the surface, but in the turbid waters below lurked unknowable slime and disease.

"I've been eating heartily," Rosemary lied. Eating had become a near-intolerable chore. She only bothered with it when her stomach began to gnaw and growl. Dorian dreaded the sight of a skeletal girl. When he'd sat for her he had often eyed her full figure with approval. Occasionally, he suggested that she could stand to gain several pounds. Whenever she was around him, she was so nervous as to devastate her appetite, but on the few occasions they had lunched together, she'd made a point of scarfing down everything her plate.

She would have carried on fictitiously about how much she loved to eat, but Dorian had lost interest. He stared out the window that looked onto the back patio. Everything there was gray and wet. Rosemary was anxious. She both wanted his attention and wanted to get out of the dining room which felt haunted by Dorian's . . . what was it, gloom?

She stood up and clapped her hands.

"Shall we find the absolutely perfect place to hang your portrait?" she asked, and started toward the door.

Dorian's eyes followed her, but he made no move to get up.

"Come on," she said, suddenly excited to show him her work, knowing that it was all the more beautiful in its elegant frame. She held a hand out to him. He looked at it, stood up, but did not accept. Still, there was a promise as he stood that he would join her.

He shadowed her down the stairs. She kept feeling the urge to look back at him, so heavy was the sensation of his gaze upon her, but she talked her way through it. The whole way down she chatted about how much she loved how the painting had turned out and how grateful she was that he had agreed to sit for her. She doubted Dorian was paying the least attention and was glad of it.

She unwrapped and lifted it quickly, her arms still aching from lugging it across town.

"Where is your fireplace?" she asked of Dorian as he met her in the foyer.

"Which one?" he said.

Rosemary laughed. Dorian did not.

"Alright, where is the largest one?" she asked, switching out of her playful tone.

Dorian raised his eyebrows in the direction of what appeared to be the main dining hall. Rosemary proceeded ahead of him.

There was a magnificent marble table chaired for over a dozen, with matching Oriental vases all down it bursting with fresh flowers. Oh, how she would like to sit at the head of that table, Mrs. Dorian Gray! At the end of the room was the fireplace. It was lifeless of course, because of the season, but oh, Rosemary imagined it churned quite the fire in the winter!

"What about up here?" she cried, leaning the painting against the mantle. No art dwelled there, and it was an ideal place for a portrait. *Destiny*, she thought. *This painting is destined to live here, in the most splendid space of all.*

"Dorian!" she called. Her voice boomeranged back at her in an echo that revealed her to be diminutive and frightened. She closed her eyes in an effort to conjure courage, and went on. "A nice roaring fire and your splendid form above it! If perhaps your valet would assist, we could hang it up and see what it is like!"

Dorian stepped into the dining room. He walked toward her slowly, with a heaviness quite contrary to his typically light and boyish gait. A strange darkness still hung over his face. Rosemary went on chattering about light, and frames, and wall space. But all she could think about was his nearness. He came to stand right beside her. His scent was sweet and musky—intoxicating. In her dreams, she breathed it in and was wondrously infused with life.

"Why did you come today?" asked Dorian, turning to her darkly.

Rosemary felt herself turning beet-red. Was she so transparent? *Well, look at yourself,* she thought, frowning at her tattered smock. *And your frantic entrance! Ha! You flung yourself in looking about ready to lie down on railroad tracks.*

"I came to give you the painting, Dorian," she said. "I came because I can't have it in my studio for a moment longer. I can't have it anywhere near me."

Dorian remained perfectly calm. Oh, he was always so wonderfully calm! It helped her articulate her crazed thoughts.

"Dorian, from the moment I met you, your personality has had the most extraordinary influence over me," she said, nodding. Yes, she must keep going. It was time to tell the truth. *Let the world lie to me,* she thought, *but I shan't lie in return.*

"I was dominated—soul, brain, and power—by you. You became to me the visible incarnation of that unseen ideal whose memory haunts us artists like an exquisite dream. I worshipped you. I grew jealous of everyone to whom you spoke. Helen, oh, Helen! I shall never forgive her for stealing you from me, but that is another matter. I wanted to have you all to myself. That has been my only want since I laid eyes upon you. I am only happy when I am with you. When you are away from me, I live in unbearable desire. These dreams of you—of things you do to me, err, things we do together— they possess my life both waking and not. Of course, I never let you know anything about this because I hardly understood it myself. I only knew that I had seen perfection face-to-face, and that the world had become wonderful to my eyes—too wonderful, perhaps, for in such mad worships there is peril, the peril of losing. . . . Weeks and weeks passed, and I grew more and more absorbed in you. For so long I have been hiding from what I know, but there is no point in hiding from it any longer."

In a leap of bravery, she grabbed his hands, clutching them to her heart. Unable to yet look in his eyes for fear of the rejection that could be dwelling there, she kept her focus on his hands, imagined them tearing through her chemise as they did in her dreams.

"Perhaps Helen is right!" she cried. "It is a far greater sin to deny our nature than to let it be free!"

"That Helen," he said, with a cruel ripple of laughter. "Helen spends her days in saying what is incredible and her evenings in doing what is improbable."

"You're starting to sound like her," said Rosemary. She regretted bringing Helen up. Already she felt stifled, choked, as if Helen were standing behind Dorian, making mocking faces at her.

"I talked to Helen about my infatuation with you, Dorian, and she just laughed at me. I didn't mind it then, so accustomed was I to her taunting me, but after she took you from me, I realized that, no, I won't be the meek mouse in this while she stalks you like a cat. I don't know what you've done together, but looking at you now, so alienated and despondent, I know it can't have been good. Oh, as if anything Helen does is good! She strives for the very opposite!"

She was nearing hysterics again. Why must she fixate on Helen? Here she was holding her beloved's hands—and he wasn't pulling away!

"Perhaps I have been foolish in imagining that there was anything between us beyond friendship. If I am so foolish, you must not be angry with me, Dorian, for what I have told you."

Biting her lower lip as she knew he liked, she at last brought her eyes to Dorian's. She was surprised by what was looking back at her in those gray, hooded eyes: sheer, primal hunger. His hands were still clutched against her when he wiggled them loose and felt her breasts freely.

"Dorian," she said, both uncertain and completely certain of where this was going.

He brought a finger to her lips.

"Shh."

With slow, predatory caution, he regarded her mouth, his finger tracing the curves of her lips.

"I've thought about this moment, Rosemary," he said. His other hand was now slid fully into her cleavage, gently kneading the ample, milk-white flesh. Her knickers felt on fire, and she closed her eyes, letting herself get lost in the ways of his touch. He leaned forward, and she felt his breath on her lips. She quivered in suspense. But he did not kiss her.

"No one has ever made love to you, is that so, Rosemary?"

She nodded rapidly. He could ask her anything and she would tell him the truth—as long as he just kept touching her. His hand circled her nipple and it stiffened, became alert. He brought his mouth to her ear and lightly licked her earlobe. She let out a small whimper of arousal at the feel of his tongue.

"Would you like me to make love to you?" he asked in a low whisper.

She nodded again. What was happening? She'd waited so long, she thought she would wait forever. And this was indecent! They were not married; he wasn't even courting her. *I am so sorry, God!* But, oh, as he tugged delicately on her hard nipple, nuptial statuses really ceased to matter.

"Come," he said, and fishing his hand out of her bodice, took her hand. He led her back up the stairs, but this time they turned into the left wing of the house and entered a magnificent bedroom. Oh, my, she was in his bedroom! It was as large and lavish as she had dreamed it would be, with flowing satin curtains along the beveled bay windows. In the center of it was the bed itself. It was not as tidy as she had dreamed it would be. The covers were tousled about. Usually they didn't look that way until the end of her dream.

He led her to the bed where she sat, somewhat awkwardly, on the very edge.

"Just a moment," he said, and abruptly left the room.

So this was it. Dorian was going to take her. At last her dreams were to come true! But the dark stuff of her dreams . . . the times when he tied her down or gagged her with knotted cloth and spanked her . . . that wasn't going to take place, was it? No, such terror would be an unbearable crime! Surely, it was just the stuff of nightmares. People didn't really do that. Well, maybe in Helen's world they did, but this was their world now: hers and Dorian's.

Watching the dying storm through the curtains, she heard him talking in the hall with the valet.

"Victor," he said, "Would you fetch me the red towels?"

"Sorry, Monsieur?" replied the valet.

"I don't know where you've put them. They were a gift from Lady Henry Wotton. A beautiful set."

"Ah, yes!" said Victor. "I had them laundered. They are just over here, Monsieur."

Their footsteps pattered down the hall.

Rosemary crossed her legs and chomped down on her lower lip. *A gift from Helen?* In her mind flashed the napkin he'd used at breakfast. Helen had a set of napkins with the same design, though it bore the initials H. W., of course. What a devil that Helen Wotton was, showering Dorian with gifts, seducing him with a wealth that had come to her by way of a faithless marriage!

Dorian appeared in the doorframe holding the sought-after Helen Wotton-tainted red towel. The sexual mood had not deserted him. His eyes grazed her voraciously.

"May I?" he asked.

Not knowing what she was acquiescing to, Rosemary nodded. Thinking about Helen had upset her, and she was no longer feeling very sensual. But that changed when Dorian came over to the bed. All he had to do was nudge her hip gently—motioning her to scoot to one side—and a bolt of lust fluttered between her legs. Dorian drew the rumpled covers down and spread the towel flatly on the mattress.

Rosemary's heart thudded in anticipation. *This is it*, she thought. *This is what you've been waiting for! How foolish of you to think you could repress the desire into obsoleteness! You need him, and maybe he needs you, too. Oh! To be needed by Dorian would be Paradise!*

Dorian took her hands and kissed them worshipfully. A lock of golden hair fell over his eye and feeling exquisitely liberated, she brushed it away. He looked at her with a spellbinding intensity. Gone was the lighthearted gaiety of the Dorian she'd painted.

"Lie down," he instructed. She obeyed, and he began undressing her. Oh, if only she were wearing a more appropriate outfit.

"You're trembling," he said.

"I'm sorry," she replied without thinking. She wanted to apologize for everything—she felt so fragile and ready to be devoured.

"You're frightened," he said.

"No, not all!" she cried. "No, I'm just—I don't really know how this goes. I know there will be pain."

"There will be, at first," he said, expertly undoing the strings of her corset. "Then there will be great pleasure."

She felt the perfect roundness of her breasts as they were freed from her chemise. Dorian grazed them lightly with his fingertips.

"You are superb, Rosemary."

He moved his hands down to her waist and slowly slid her knickers down. Her vagina was fully exposed, moistening under his marveling gaze. He looked at her as if she were a work of genius art.

"I am going to kiss every part of your body, Rosemary," he said quietly. "Would you like that?"

"Yes!" she gasped, surprised at how shrill her voice sounded.

"Good," he said. "Where would you like me to kiss you first?"

Rosemary bit her lower lip and blushed.

"*Mmm*," he said. "You want me to kiss you there." He leaned his face close to hers, and tilted her chin up.

"Have you ever been kissed by a man?" he asked.

She hesitated, then shook her head. Before she could feel any shame, he kissed her tenderly on the mouth. His lips were warm and soft. He took his time, until by her own will, she opened her mouth slightly. She felt his tongue slide along the inner parts of her lips then find hers and rouse it into a gentle play. She was kissing him back with passion. *This is it*, she thought, *this is kissing*! With each locking and unlocking of their tongues, Rosemary felt the craving between her thighs intensify.

He broke away from the kiss and moved on to her neck, first kissing then suckling with a most pleasing thirst. One hand held the back of her head while the other rubbed her breast. A moan escaped her lips when his hand went lower, down the length of her abdomen, and stopped a mere inch above her vagina. It ached for his touch.

"There," she said. "Please touch me there."

"Be patient," said Dorian, muffled in kisses. With diligence and skill, he kissed along her breasts, pausing to suck a nipple. Rosemary shuddered in ecstasy, moaning louder. He drew his tongue the length of her stomach. When he curled his tongue along her navel, she squealed with delight. Would he kiss her there? Yes. *Ah!* She had to bite her lip to keep from crying out. He was kissing her there.

Was ever there such an exquisite sensation? His tongue at first skimmed the folds of flesh, then delved in, lapping up her juices. Reflexively, Rosemary's back arched and her calves stiffened. A most enthralling sensation was building in her. Dorian's tongue moved more rapidly and came to focus on the aching center, the raised ball of nerves at the top of her mound. As he lingered there, she cried out in ecstatic agony. He stopped abruptly, and she felt she would die if he did not bring her to the explosion she was so nearing.

In all of this, Dorian was still fully dressed. Just then he stood and began to disrobe, removing his shirt and pants without the least bit of shame. And considering the sheer beauty of his body, there was no reason for anything but the utmost pride. He was so tall and broad, and every muscle in his chest was accentuated, exercised to perfection. As he removed his underwear, Rosemary stared in awe, the unfulfilled aching in her pussy rising to a near painful intensity. She had seen dirty daguerreotypes before—Helen had a sizable collection—but none of the penises depicted there had been as enormous as this one. Rosemary realized why his hands were so large and handsome—to pair with this master cock. She felt a very important part of Dorian had been left out of her portrait.

Deep as her aching for it was, she was worried at first whether it would fit in her, and if it did, would it damage her in some way? He walked over to the bed, his cock sticking straight up like a sword. He was about to impale her!

In a sudden frenzy, Rosemary wrapped the towel around herself.

"Are you nervous?" he asked, holding his cock and massaging it with more force than Rosemary thought necessary. He was but a foot away from her.

"Yes," she said. Her voice was so meek, she felt barely audible. What was she doing? Here was the beautiful Dorian Gray flawlessly naked before her, handling the very thing she'd longed to have inside of her for months, and she was overcome with cowardice. She covered her eyes with her hands.

"It's all right," he said softly, and came closer. He lowered one of her hands from her face and, with her eyes still closed, brought her hand down to touch him. Rosemary took a deep, empowering breath, and let go of the towel.

It was warm, warmer than it had been in her dreams. He wrapped her hand around it—or as much as was possible, because her hand was too small to encircle it. He moved her hand slowly back and forth. She opened her eyes and looked up at him. His eyes were fixed on hers, but there was a look of delirium seeping into his expression.

"Yes, keep doing that," he said, letting go. She continued jerking him softly.

"You can apply more pressure," he said. She tightened her grip.

"And a little faster," he said. She complied.

"That feels very good. Now, don't so much pull the whole thing, just the skin. Yes, that's good. *Mmmm.* Keep it light and fast. Now, with your other hand," he said, taking her free hand and placing it on his scrotum. He guided her fingers into the moist, hairy sac, bringing her hand to cup one ball that her palm could barely contain. Then he brought her hand to the other right beside it. She knew these were the testicles in which lay a man's procreative seed, but she had not known they were a source of pleasure. They, too, seemed untenably large. She wondered how all of this didn't show through his pants.

"Rub them," he said.

She complied, rubbing in the same manner she rubbed the shaft.

"No," he said, and she let go completely and looked up at him at a loss. Was she terrible at this? She felt perhaps it would be best to stop.

"I mean, it feels good. You are still learning. Now, when you tug on my balls, you can go a little harder. They can take it."

She went back to it. Soon she had developed a rhythm, her right hand loosely jerked his cock, while her left vigorously massaged his balls. Dorian's head tilted back in pleasure. "Ah, that's good," he said. "Now, stop, stop!" he ordered.

She let go, and surrendered her hands in the air. This time she knew he wasn't stopping her because what she was doing did not feel good, but because, to the contrary, it felt too good. Just as she'd been ready to explode when he was licking and sucking her, she was bringing him too close to the sun. She wanted to pat herself on the back. *You're doing it*, she thought. *You're pleasing your Lord, a God among men, Dorian Gray!*

"Lie down," he said, and she fell back against the pillows, naked before him, the red towel beneath her.

"You've got a bit of paint on your neck," he said, touching it lightly. "One of these days, I should like to use a paintbrush and some paint on your naked body. I sense we could have some enjoyment in that. I should like to begin right here," he said, bringing his hand down to her vagina, tugging a wet tendril of hair. The sensation made her crazy and Rosemary involuntarily thrust upward.

"I think you are ready," Dorian said.

Ah, yes, thought Rosemary. *I am ready, so ready.*

Dorian got on top of her and kissed her long and deep. He put his hands on her thighs and pulled them apart, further and further. She was no longer afraid of his enormous cock. No, she was anything but afraid. She was eager for it. She would die without it. And just then, she felt it begin its deep plunge inside her. Then it was filling her up, and filling her up some more. She cried out. Her walls were caving around it.

"Relax," whispered Dorian. And then it was in deeper and he was mounting her slowly, generously, kissing her neck as he did. She felt his cock pushing against her maidenhead, prying for entry, and then *snap*! All that fuss was over with. The seal was broken, met with an onrush of unthinkable pain. Rosemary yelped and dug her fingernails into Dorian's shoulders. He kept thrusting without mercy, his hands holding her breasts, squeezing her hard nipples. His cock was all the way in now, moving in and further into her. Rosemary felt all of her existing right there, between her pussy and his cock, and miraculously the pain began to melt away, and with each mount she felt a building inside her—this one deeper and more intense than the climaxing from when he was licking her. Oh, she didn't know what was going to happen, but it was *going* to happen. She dug deeper into his shoulders, dimly aware that she was screaming.

"Yes, yes, oh, God," she howled.

"Yes, Rosemary," he said, kissing her furiously. "Yes, you are going to come."

"Yes!" she cried. And all at once her thoughts disappeared as he rode her to the top of the world, where for a moment she hung suspended, her cries muffled in his shoulder, and then, ah, she fell stupendously from the magnificent height, crashing down into an orgasm that saw no limits.

"Oh!" she cried, her mind spinning, overpowered by the ecstasy. Dorian kept thrusting as her furious aching subsided around him. She was out of breath, practically limp. Dorian was still hard as steel inside her, fucking her relentlessly, when abruptly he pulled out.

"Roll over," he said.

She opened her eyes. Her vision was hazy, drugged with satisfaction.

"Hmm?" she murmured.

"On your stomach," he said, scooping her up by the hips as if she weighed no more than a doll, and plopping her onto her belly. Within a moment, he was back inside of her, plowing rigorously away. This was less thrilling for the inside of her vagina, but the weight of him upon her mashed the front of her pussy into the mattress so that, in a position familiar to her from her lonely nights, her clitoris was stimulated.

"You like that?" asked Dorian.

"Mmm," Rosemary moaned into the pillow, embarking on another climax.

"You like when I fuck you hard?"

Rosemary moaned again in response, though only half paying attention.

"You like it when I punish you?" he asked, digging his cock into her, speeding up, going so fast she felt she may break—and not in the pleasurable sense. Then all of a sudden, *slap!* Her bottom rang out in pain. Then another, and another. He kept slapping her. She was too confused at first to register, and by the time she understood—he was beating her—she was crying hot tears into the pillow, and then she was wailing.

"Stop it!" she cried. "Stop!"

And he did stop, but now he had his hands around her neck and was squeezing the life out of her. She fought his fingers with her own tiny ones, and started to gag.

"Ahhh!" yelled Dorian, and she felt his cock spasm within her and then he quickly pulled out. He released her at last. A rush of warm fluid spewed onto her welted bottom, as she pulled air into her lungs.

"Ah, yes," Dorian said, kissing her head, while he ran his hands along her sides. "Oh, Rosemary, you feel so perfect. So tight and new. I could fuck you forever."

Rosemary was silent, gathering the courage to say what? To do what? She was stricken. Her dreams had been all too prophetic. Dorian Gray wanted to hurt her—he *had* hurt her.

He rolled over beside her, panting, then touched her shoulder, indicating she turn onto her back. She remained with her head in the pillow.

"Rosemary?" he said.

She did not want him to hear her crying. Or maybe she did. She was unsure what she wanted. Perhaps she wanted nothing to do with him. Yes, for now, she had to get away.

Holding the towel against her breasts, she stood. Her legs quaked, the muscles exhausted. There was incredible soreness in her vagina, like a spiked fist was inside her, and it was a challenge to walk. She looked down and saw trails of blood on her inner thighs. She dropped the towel. The imperious red of the fabric camouflaged her virgin blood but she felt it drenched in one area.

"Rosemary?" said Dorian again, a hint of worry in his voice.

"What?" she said, recovering from her tears.

"Where are you going?"

She dressed quickly, not bothering with all the under-garments, just her chemise and knickers. She couldn't be seen in public like this, and would have to get into a hansom immediately.

"Please have Victor—that's his name, right? Please have Victor get me a hansom. I must go at once."

"But Rosemary," said Dorian, leaping up and rushing to her side. He was still naked, and Rosemary had not the courage to look at him, at that thing that had been inside her.

He grabbed her hands and held them to his lips in a near-dozen kisses, looking at her imploringly. His eyes were no longer filled with the grave absence, but were lively and bright again. They reminded her of the eyes she'd painted.

"Talk to me," he said.

"You're cruel," she murmured.

"What?" he said, appearing quite shocked.

"Cruel!" she cried. "You're cruel! A barbarian!"

"But Rosemary," he pleaded.

"No!" she said. "No, and I mean no. Do not try and speak to me about this now. I want to leave at once."

She fought the tears back and ignored the beautiful, hurt face before her—the face of her Lord, her master. It was all too much to take in, and she thought she may faint if she did not leave at once. The source of all her passions and love was revealed to be brutal.

"Do not see me out," she said. Dorian looked too stricken to argue.

On her way out, she passed through the living room where the painting lay in abandon by the fireplace. *Burn it*, she thought, but she did not go near it. She glimpsed Victor in the main hall, opening the door for her, and wearing the falsest of smiles with tears seeping through, she hobbled wretchedly out onto the busy street where everything seemed just as it had been when she last saw it, but so much wetter.

CHAPTER VII

For some reason or the other, the theater was crowded that night, and the fat manager who met them at the door was beaming from ear to ear with an oily, tremulous smile. He escorted Helen and Dorian to their box with a sort of pompous humility, waving his fat jeweled hands, and talking at the top of his voice.

Once they were settled in their private compartment with a central view of the stage, Dorian looked around with an abundance of satisfaction. He quite admired Helen's capacity for decadence. And he was all the more impressed that it was a woman impressing him. Then again, it was her husband's riches she was squandering. In the past few weeks since meeting Helen, he'd pondered just how much money must Lord Wotton withdraw from his account to appease her, and why was he so benevolent? Dorian resolved to ask Rosemary about the situation, as he expected it would be quite a juicy tale.

"You say your husband doesn't have a taste for theater?" Dorian said, testing the subject.

"No," said Helen, tersely. "I said my husband doesn't have taste."

"Oh," he said, and resigned himself to asking no more questions about Lord Henry Wotton. It may have been in his best interests not to know enough to sympathize with the fellow, anyway, given that he had fucked his wife in his own carriage not long ago.

It was early yet, and the lights were bright in the auditorium. The audience had taken off their waistcoats and hung them over their chairs. They talked to each other across the theater. Some tawdry women were laughing in the pit. Their voices were horribly shrill and discordant. The sound of the popping of corks came from the bar.

"Do you like any of them?" asked Helen.

"Pardon?" said Dorian, flipping idly through the playbill.

"The girls," said Helen, indicating the throngs of made-up women below with a comprehensive wave of her hand.

Dorian thought to feign innocence as to what Helen was getting at—he was still reluctant to be in such public presence with this sorceress of sin. Usually they met in private, or at an hour so late no one of worth would recognize or remember that they were together. He quarreled with himself. Why should he be ashamed? What use was there in pretending he wasn't on the hunt for degradation? And who would argue that Helen Wotton wasn't the most suitable chaperone? He accepted the opera glasses from Helen and scanned the audience.

Women of all ages were well gussied up for a night on the town, their hair spun up and pinned on the top of their heads, trapped in place by sparkling jeweled pins and long velvet ribbons. There were some definite beauties among them, but whenever his eyes fell upon a small, dark-haired girl, his heart raced. He hoped it would be Rosemary. But every time he caught sight of her face, the eyes were too close together, or the nose was too snubbed, or the mouth was too thin, or there was any other combination of features that spelled out: stranger—a creature of lesser beauty. It was hopeless and painful, and, he wondered, would the feeling ever leave? He'd been positively heartsick since Rosemary left. He'd sent her letters defending himself and even went to her house, where he was greeted coldly by her butler and told that Rosemary was not at home. Dorian stuck his head in the doorway, peering frantically around, calling her name. He could feel her presence, but the butler refused him entry and bade him to leave lest he notify the police of a trespasser.

Ah, looking around for the next woman for him to entertain his sexual fancies was not what he wanted. But he would not waste his fleeting youth and virility poeticizing Rosemary Hall and pining for her in chastity. No, he'd keep himself sated and empty his seed on a regular basis.

"Some of them are nice," he said to Helen.

"Nice?" said Helen. She yawned loudly.

"Well, there are some beautiful ones," considered Dorian, continuing to roam the audience through the optical lenses. It felt wrong to be looking at decent women this way, like they were pets that were up for purchase.

"What about the one in the yellow dress with the red hair?" said Helen, then murmured in his ear, "Don't be afraid to skip past the ugly ones. The old and tired had their time. They've been plucked and now can only wither. Like every fruit and flower, humans, too, go bad and rot."

Dorian frowned through the glasses. There was more than one redhead, but he couldn't spot any in a yellow dress . . . and then there she was. A tall, slender girl with a surprisingly curvy physique and hair as fiery as a burning sun. He recognized her at once.

"Ah, I know that one!" he exclaimed.

"Ah, you do?" said Helen with some intrigue. "She's a magnificent-looking creature. Where did you come across her?"

"I will tell you, Helen, but you mustn't be unsympathetic about it," he warned, for she could get very jealous when she was excluded from anything that bore even a taste of the libidinous.

"After all," he went on. "It never would have happened if I had not met you. You filled me with a wild desire to know everything about life. For days after I met you, something seemed to throb in my veins. I had a passion for sensations. . . . Well, one evening at about seven o'clock, I was determined to go out in search of some adventure. I felt that this gray monstrous London of ours, with its myriads of people, its sordid sinners, and its splendid sins, as you once phrased it, must have something in store for me. I fancied a thousand things. The mere danger gave me a sense of delight. I remembered what you had said to me on that wonderful evening when we first dined together, about the search for beauty being the real secret of life. I don't know what I expected, but I went out and wandered eastward, soon losing my way in a labyrinth of grimy streets and black grassless squares. About half past eight I passed by an absurd little theater, with great flaring gas jets and gaudy playbills. You will laugh at me, I know, but I really went in and paid a whole guinea for the stage box. But, oh, the night I had! It was so worth remembering that I vowed to forget it immediately lest I tarnish its luster."

As he spoke, Helen watched him with a look of pride on her face, like a mother whose son has come home after a long time away to deliver her his riches. She could take credit for all the changes in him. His nature had developed like a flower, had born blossoms of scarlet flame. He was no longer the restrained, inexperienced boy that Helen had met in Rosemary's studio. Out of its hiding place had crept his soul, and desire had come to meet it on the way. That pleased Helen, which in part pleased Dorian, given that he felt oddly compelled to obey her, as if she were a Goddess who would ruin him if he didn't earn her enchantments.

But since the incident with Rosemary, he'd felt conflicted. There was great fun in being sinful, in sucking from the nectar of youth before it ran out, but at what cost? He'd been cruel to Rosemary, deflowered her in a rage of greed, taking advantage of her vulnerable love for him. And yet, curiously enough, he'd felt a love for her, too. As he started making love to her, he'd wanted to excite and fulfill her. It wasn't until the end of their lovemaking that a darkness had roused in him and he heard Helen's maddening orders to punish without mercy.

She sighed with contentment.

"There are exquisite things in store for you," said Helen. "This is merely the beginning. Tell me, who is the divine redhead?"

"Her name is Sybil Vane."

"Never heard of her," said Helen.

"I'm afraid it may remain that way," said Dorian. "She's a mediocre actress—too mediocre to be terrible, in fact. She merely blends in with the dreadful scenery."

Helen laughed at the sound of her own wisdom coming out of Dorian's mouth. Like any disease looking to thrive, it was good news to be contagious.

"My dear," she began. "No tawdry girl like that could be anything but mediocre. She's designed to be a decorative sex object. Girls like her never have anything to say, but they say it charmingly."

Dorian considered Helen's words. He thought of how beautiful Rosemary was, with eyes so blue they could color the sky; her bashful smile; her chestnut hair that fell like dark leaves around her pale, heart-shaped face. There was something of the fawn in her shy grace and startled eyes.

The curves of her throat were the curves of a white lily. Her cool, ivory hands around his hard cock had been so delicate and willing to learn.

"There are beautiful women who are also geniuses," said Dorian, returning the glasses to Helen's lap. "Do you think my nature so shallow?"

"No, I think your nature so deep. My dear Dorian, I am analyzing women at present for the very motive of your pleasure. But you seem to gaze upon these gazelles as potential players in actual conversation. For that sport, there are only a few women in London worth talking to, and you're talking to one of them now."

"What about Rosemary?" he asked. "Would you relegate her to the lowly majority, or does she get residence in your high quarters?"

"Rosemary is a fine painter," Helen said. "She can articulate a paintbrush wondrously. But she puts everything that is charming in her into her work. The consequence is that she has nothing left for life but her prejudices, her principles, and her pitifully common sense. The only artists I have ever known who are personally delightful are bad artists. Good artists exist simply in what they make, and consequently, are perfectly uninteresting in what they are. A great poet, a really great poet, is the most unpoetical of all creatures. But inferior poets are absolutely fascinating. The worse their rhymes are, the more picturesque they look. The mere fact of having published a book of second-rate sonnets makes one quite irresistible. Such a person lives the poetry that he cannot write. The others write the poetry that they dare not realize. Rosemary is no exception. Why, the picture she painted of you! All her desires turned to oil."

Dorian shook his head. To hear of Rosemary discussed this way was maddening. He couldn't remember ever having felt so defensive of—nor intrigued by—someone. He thought of Rosemary's little animal screams as he plunged into her, and how she'd writhed under his mouth when he feasted between her thighs, moving her closer and closer to oblivion. How sweet she had tasted. And what desires she had—turned to oil, perhaps, but also to sexual juices that had run down his lips and chin. Helen had no idea!

"Rosemary has not merely art in her, but she has personality also, and you have often told me that it is personalities, not principles, that move the age."

"Yes, that does sound like something I would say," said Helen. She was distracted, fishing around in her reticule. She withdrew a plump cigarette.

"You fucked her, didn't you?" said Helen.

Dorian felt his mouth drop open. Well, she had some idea, alright.

"Oh, the scandal of it all," mocked Helen. She lit the cigarette and sucked with a hiss. The musky smell of opium enveloped them.

"You must have a cigarette," continued Helen. "A cigarette is the perfect type of a perfect pleasure. It is exquisite, and it leaves one unsatisfied."

She held the case out to him.

"How did you know?" he asked.

"You haven't learned how to keep a secret yet," she said.

Dorian frowned. "I didn't say a word to anyone."

Helen smirked and held a finger to his lips. "Not here," she said. "Here," and dabbed the middle of his forehead with two pointed fingers. "Your eyes say it all."

Dorian was dumbfounded. Helen offered the cigarette case to him again.

"Your cigarettes are always a bit dangerous," said Dorian, not wanting to become as obliterated as he had the last time he'd been to see Sybil Vane perform. "May I have one that is just tobacco?"

"I'm sorry, but when I go to the theater, I prepare for the greatest of boredoms. You'll have to make do with these. Here, take this one—it's thin."

Dorian accepted. Before making Helen's acquaintance, he never much cared for smoking, but now he ardently enjoyed it. Within the first inhalation, he felt a fuzzy calm lay into his brain. The touch of opium made clay of his senses, rolling them into a sluggish blob.

"Tell me about the actress," Helen said, making no secret of the fact that hearing such flattering talk about Rosemary disagreed with her. "Was she worth the trouble? Would you like to try her again?"

"I didn't try her at all," Dorian said, agitation managing to poke its way through the haze. "After the performance, I took up with a group of charming monsters and by the time I parted with them I was so addled with opium that I had trouble collecting myself for pursuit. When I got to her dressing room, she was gone."

"Hmm," considered Helen. "She is beautiful, and the initial sight of her ignited in me a wicked curiosity. I must say, my dear, I'm craving a taste of her."

Dorian had to agree—she was lovely to behold. A faint blush, like the shadow of a rose in a mirror of silver, came to her cheeks as she glanced at the crowded enthusiastic house. She stepped back a few paces, and her lips seemed to tremble.

The scene was the hall of Capulet's house, and Romeo in his pilgrim's dress had entered with Mercutio and his other friends. The band struck up a few bars of music, and the dance began. Through the crowd of ungainly, shabbily dressed actors, Sybil Vane moved like a creature from a finer world. Her body swayed while she danced, as a plant sways in the water.

"She is quite beautiful, Dorian," murmured Helen.

"Mm-hmm," said Dorian with a slight nod. Dimly, he thought of what he would like to do to her, but his thoughts—the things beneath the haze, calling him back to himself—were only of Rosemary. It could be that she would never see or speak to him again. What could he do? For starters, he would hang the painting above the mantle, as she'd wished. Yes, it was the perfect place for it. Why had he been so stubborn? He was ill with a hangover that day, and so many poisons had yet to leave his system when she'd shown up looking like she'd broken out of a madhouse. Ah, but still, she had been beautiful and had moved him to new heights of feeling.

As it were, Sybil Vane moved much finer than she acted. As an actress, she was curiously listless. She showed no sign of joy when her eyes rested on Romeo. The staginess of her acting was unbearable, and grew worse as she went on. Her gestures became absurdly artificial. She over-emphasized everything she had to say. The other actors weren't much better, and ultimately, the play was a fiasco that just dragged on and on interminably. To concentrate on the scenes being painfully doled out onstage was to risk brain damage, and so Dorian smoked another laced cigarette, this one of medium width.

Half of the audience that left during intermission never returned, tramping out in heavy boots and laughing. The last act was played to almost empty benches. The curtain went down on a titter and some groans.

"Ha!" laughed Helen, amused. "What a farce!"

"Yes, I guess she actually is terrible, in fact," said Dorian. He was feeling tired and removed from his surroundings. He longed to be at home. His wish to hang up the painting, to honor Rosemary's fine work, had persisted.

"I suppose I should like to go home now," he said to Helen, knowing she would be displeased. "I've some things I'd like to take care of."

Helen scoffed. "And miss the best part of the play?"

"Pardon?" said Dorian.

"Dorian," said Helen, reaching her arm around him with authority. "The best part of the play is when the play is over. Now don't be daft. Let's go get some Sybil Vane."

Dorian laughed. The theater swirled around him. He was more affected by the opium than he'd thought. Helen's eyes seemed very large, and very black. All the various greens and browns and golds of her irises had fallen into her expansive pupils.

"Are you serious?" asked Dorian.

"I hope to never be serious, Dorian," she said, then laughed. "What does it matter if she plays Juliet like a wooden doll? She is very lovely, and if she knows as little about life as she does about acting, she will be a delightful experience for us. There are only two kinds of people who are really fascinating: people who know absolutely everything, and people who know absolutely nothing."

Dorian shrugged. He wasn't wholly convinced, but perhaps Helen had a point. They were already out, after all, and they'd just sat through two hours of worthless performances.

"In our play, she won't be so dreadful, I assure you," said Helen.

Dorian chuckled. It was all just a play, wasn't it? He looked around the empty theater. The audience had merely left one play for another, that of their own lives.

"Well?" said Helen, losing patience. "Do you not believe a most entertaining play can be arranged?"

"I have total faith in your boldness, Helen," said Dorian, shaking his head and smiling. The barking of his conscience had finally ceased.

"Terrific," said Helen. "Now, let's eat! Oh, I know, I know, you think we had a full meal before we came here. Ha!" She slapped his hand. "That was only a starter course!"

CHAPTER VIII

Backstage, the air was thick with smoke and rumbling with loud, divergent chatter. Everyone seemed to be talking at once and to no one in particular. It was randomness and chaos and every now and again a perfect harmony was born of it. Dorian was excited to be a member of such a late-night choir of dissonance, in which sex and sordidness felt both the origin and the destination. Helen was an expert in navigating the crowd. She hooked arms with Dorian, and together they slithered through the crowd like eels.

"What a place to find one's divinity!" cried Helen, winking as she broke away from him and sunk into the sea of smoke and men. She remained out of sight for a long while.

Dorian soon found himself in fragmented talk with some of the actors from the play. Aside from an untucked shirt here or a loosened suspender there, the men were essentially still in costume. To be up close and talking to them as men rather than as characters was disillusioning. They were like impostors; their smiling, natural faces were devilishly unreal, and Romeo was just an average ruffian who talked speedily about a "pre-arranged" and "upcoming" trip to America that was obviously neither. A black, hairy mole took liberty on the tip his nose. It summarized him in a sad way.

Dorian sought sympathy in a bottle of gin that was being passed around. A couple of the actors were talking about going to a men's club, and Dorian had halfway agreed to join them when he felt a tug on his shirt cuff. He turned around and there was Helen, smiling broadly at him, a smug twinkle in the blackness of her eyes.

"There you are," he said.

"Busy?" she asked.

Dorian shook his head.

"Bored," he replied. "I'm soon to head out to a club, I think."

"You may want to postpone that," said Helen.

Dorian frowned. How Helen dreaded this time of the night, when her rowdy companions trotted off to vile, stinking places where she was not permitted entry. He felt a strange compassion for her, this soul who had been miscast as the fairer sex, when she was as swarthy and rugged as any brute. The most prestigious women's clubs of London kept their innocuous reading rooms stocked with romance novels, and their bed chambers virginal and immaculate to appeal to the virtues of a woman of her wealth and position. The finest boutiques swung open their doors in the hopes that a lady as spendthrift as she would buy their soaps and petticoats. She could have anything she wanted, but the frills and flowers and gasp-worthy price tags that sent the hearts of the most sophisticated women

squirreling into a most unsophisticated squall left Helen
unfazed at best, but often insulted. The objects of her desire lived in the smoking parlors and the men's clubs; they
didn't bear any designer label or cashmere, or pearl. These
objects, in fact, were not objects at all; they were actions
representing freedom, and they were not for women to
touch.

Dorian knew how badly she wanted to be a part of a
man's devil-may-care world. He perceived her as a kind of
vampire in reverse: banished to the day, to dress fittings, to
teatime, and to gardens being coaxed into year-round blossom. He pitied her sometimes. How peculiar it was to be
friends with a woman. Everything in society complicated,
shunned, and forbade it.

As a meager means of consolation, Dorian offered
Helen the bottle of gin that the men had been sharing. She
took a hearty swig, her eyes bent on him. She then slammed the drained bottle on a little table with such force that
the table broke. The commotion barely ruffled a feather
in the general clamor, and the spectacle, it seemed, would
soon be forgotten—until Dorian saw Romeo. When Helen
had broken the table, she had sent a bucket of melting ice
careening into Romeo's lap. He leaped up in a laughing fit,
too drunk to stand straight. He held his stomach, either
for equilibrium or to measure his need to retch, or both.
His eyes settled in a bleary squint on Helen.

"Helen Wotton!" he cried, as if her name won him a
raffle in the underworld.

"Romeo, oh, Romeo," said Helen, with a roll of her eyes.

"Ah!" he scowled, then cried out. "It's me! Alan Campbell!"

"All right," said Helen, with an air of indifference that indicated the name didn't ring a bell. This upset Romeo Alan Campbell. He shook his fist heavenward.

"You feign ignorance, Helen Wotton!" he cried, turning to the small group of men around him for sympathy. They shared a crude, confused laughter.

"Well, I suppose lying is a necessary skill in your field," said Romeo Alan Campbell.

"Lying?" said Helen. "I leave that to you. You do it so well."

Romeo Alan Campbell scoffed.

"You make the mistake of the low commoners, Helen Wotton! Acting and lying are unrelated!"

"I agree. I love acting. It is so much more real than life. But what you were doing out on stage was lying."

Romeo Alan Campbell turned a curious shade of red.

"Mr. Campbell, is there something you wish to obtain from me?" asked Helen.

Romeo Alan Campbell bit his lip, and waved to the small group of men around him.

"You know of Helen Wotton," he cried to them.

"Ah, the rich old whore!" called one of the men, who, for some reason, was dressed as a clown, with a fat red honker affixed to his nose and a tassel of painted bells strung around his neck. He saluted Dorian empty-handed.

"She'll fuck ya' blind!" cried another man in thick spectacles.

"Does she need a dressing room?" cried another, rather nonsensically. He was too short to be seen over the shoulder of Romeo Alan Campbell.

"An undressing room is what she needs," cried Romeo Alan Campbell, riling the crowd into an uproar.

Helen remained stoic, dragging coolly from her cigarette.

"Old husband, quite the moneybags," said the clown. "You can find him belly up in the gutter by Madame Stroggel's lodging house. And we all know the sort of lasses who lodge with Madame Stroggel!"

"Aye!" cheered the men, then snickering like meddling rats. Helen only smiled. On one hand, Dorian was proud of her endurance; on the other, he was appalled that she had to endure such behavior at all. He was embarrassed for her and took her aside, a gesture that made the men hoot and holler all the more.

"Is there anywhere you'd like to go?" he murmured in her ear.

Her eyes were frosty and unfocused. For the first time, Dorian was worried about her.

"Where would you like me to take you?" he asked. "Wherever you wish."

"What about the club?" she asked, clutching his arm. "Aren't you heading there shortly?"

"I want nothing to do with these boorish asses," he said. "I am your humble guest, and they are content to insult you as if it were a wicked game wherein the greatest loser wins."

Helen nodded.

"If I may just take a moment to sit down and just . . ." she said, puffing rapidly from a cigarette perilously nearing its nub.

"Of course, of course," Dorian whispered. "We shall go outside and inhale the cool, sobering breeze. Then we may go have a cup of tea somewhere. There is no need for you to be subject to all this. You are none of what they say. And Lord Wotton—while I've yet to make his acquaintance—why, his doings reflect nothing on you. Though I am not inclined to believe what they say of him."

He wanted to give her tousled, blond head a kiss but did not want her to be heckled further.

"Let's just get out of here," he said and, shielding her with his arms, escorted her out of the packed room. A brawl was beginning, and Dorian sensed that if they didn't get out quickly, they'd be cornered.

Helen murmured something inaudible as they were walking out.

"Shh," said Dorian, patting her back. "Let's just get out of here."

Poor dear! No matter the steel façade, she was beneath it, like all women, mere porcelain and pain. He squeezed her shoulder and led her toward the lobby. From there they would exit onto the main street and hail a hansom. They could find peace in a sleepy tavern nearby. He'd have a stiff Alexander. The lady would have a hot tea to calm her jangling nerves.

"No!" she cried, as if she'd heard the non-alcoholic recommendation. She jerked free of him.

"What's the matter?" Dorian asked.

Helen started toward him and put her hand on his belt and tugged until it loosened. She held the buckle teasingly and laughed at the look of surprise on his face. Her eyes were gleaming onyx. Dear God, had she gone mad? He ought to have known better than to get involved at this capacity with a woman. Women were always going mad. It was like going anywhere else for them, only they didn't announce it like they did when going to the store. They just went. One moment they were there, the next they had gone to madness, where they could stay for as long as they damn well liked.

"Helen, please stop."

She pouted like a child denied her playtime. With some strength, Dorian removed her hands.

"Let's go," he said, starting back toward the exit.

"Sybil Vane!" she cried, standing with her arms crossed. She was only one person—a woman, at that—but it looked like it would take an army to move her.

"What about her?" he asked, and then asked himself, *yes, what about her? Where had she gone? Why hadn't she made an appearance backstage?*

"I know where to find her," said Helen. Her voice was her own again, husky and sure.

"Helen, this is play will be showing for a month," said Dorian. "We can find her any night of the week. Let's get away from these jeering fools."

"No," she said, grabbing his hand. "Follow me."

She veered them down a gas-lit hall with arched medieval doors, some looking like they'd been shut for years, with rusty knobs and sodden cracks. Others were ajar with smoky light peering out. There was a woman laughing somewhere. The air was dank.

At the very end of the hall, Helen stopped before a door, which read Dressing Room on a slat of wood glued haphazardly to the top. Underneath it was a dingy chalkboard bearing, in a dusty yellow chalk, a name: Sybil Vane.

Helen stepped back and raised a brow at Dorian, leaving this task to him.

Reluctantly, he knocked.

"No, fool!" cried Helen. "Don't attract attention!"

"Pardon?" asked Dorian.

"Oh!" cried Helen, as if she were dealing with an incorrigible child. She pushed Dorian aside and gave the knob a hard turn, pushing her weight against the door until it barreled open.

It was a dressing room, indeed, although a dingy one. The wallpaper, a pale-blue paisley, was peeling, revealing crusty, water-damaged wood. The room was only big enough to hold a few people, and not comfortably. A small dressing table took up much of the space. Plates of powders and unguents covered it messily with stray brushes hanging around them. The mirror was spotted and cracked so that when someone looked in it, he became doubled and ghastly. A flickering lantern was the only source of light.

"Sybil," called Helen in a low voice. "My dear Sybil, I have brought him to you." She crept to a tall wardrobe that had cheap fabrics sticking out of its not-quite-shut doors. Helen opened them, and a crouched figure stirred. Dorian glimpsed a tendril of coppery-red hair.

"Sybil, darling," said Helen. "I promised to bring you your Prince and here he is."

Helen signaled for Dorian to come over. She held a finger over her lips, indicating silence.

"She's a wee bit timid," Helen said. "Come." She reached for Dorian's hand. Reluctantly, he gave it.

He crouched in front of the cabinet in which Sybil Vane crouched.

"She'll come around," whispered Helen in his ear, and then went to the dressing table, where she pulled out a chalice of emerald liquor—absinthe. Dorian turned to her for an explanation. She merely winked at him.

"Romeo always keeps a goblet of love potion for his Juliets," she said, pouring a glass and setting it to heat over the flickering lantern.

Dorian touched the girl's shoulder with a kind of cautious gentleness he'd only known when, as a child, he'd held his hand out to feed wild doves.

"Sybil," he said.

She turned to him. Her face was tear-streaked. There was terror in her large brown eyes. Up close he saw that her hair was dyed with henna. Her roots showed an ashy brown-blonde.

"Prince Charming?" she said, her voice cracking.

Dorian felt that if he answered, "No," the girl would become more upset. He placed a hand on her huddled knees. She was trembling.

"Yes," he said. "Yes, it is Prince Charming. Come, let's get you out of here."

He lifted his hand and held it to her. She looked at him, her lips quivering, and shook her head.

"It's all right. I can take you out of here and get you a nice meal. A hot meal. You would like that, wouldn't you?"

She nodded and looked up, trying to show him something. He followed her gaze and shrieked at what he saw. The long satin ribbon that had held her Juliet locks back was now binding her wrists to a metal spoke in the cabinet wall.

His shriek startled her and she looked at him in panic.

"No, it's fine," he said. "Let me just—" he began. "If I may unwrap this, all right?"

She did not refuse so he went into the dark, mothy cabinet. Behind him, Helen called out. "The drama, the drama," she said. "It goes on well after the curtain has fallen!"

"Helen," called Dorian, wrestling with the tie. She'd made quite a knot.

"She told me to wait for you," murmured Sybil. "She told me you would come. I saw you that night. That night at the theater. You saw me. You saw me, too. I wanted so badly for you to come and talk to me afterward. But you disappeared. I thought it too good to be true, a man like you to come to talk to me."

The girl giggled through her tears. She was either drugged or totally mad.

"Helen, what have you done?" he cried, as he finally undid the knot. With her arms free, the girl closed like a Chinese fan unto herself.

"Oh, Dorian, please," said Helen. "If you want to make a scene, the stage is out there." She stooped down to him and held out a glass of absinthe. "Careful," she warned. "Hot."

Dorian took the glass and, not knowing what to do with it, offered it to the poor girl. She grabbed it in a flash and drank.

"Good girl!" cried Helen.

Dorian turned to her. "Have you gone completely mad?" he cried.

"Get the glass back," instructed Helen.

"What?"

"You heard me," said Helen.

Frazzled, Dorian reached for the glass. Sybil handed it to him with a look of appreciation. He returned it to Helen.

"Greedy girls actresses are," said Helen, examining the empty glass.

"Helen," said Dorian, with the girl's dreamy eyes upon him. "I want to know what is going on. And I want to know now."

"I got us Sybil Vane!" cried Helen, heating up another glass.

"This is quite a way to go about it," said Dorian.

Helen clucked her tongue happily. "Isn't it, though?"

"The amount of trouble you may get into for this—" started Dorian, but Helen cut him off.

"The amount of trouble I may get into for this?" she repeated. "Me alone? Who is the Prince Charming here who has just set her free, for whom she was tied up in the first place? Now, Dorian, don't be daft. Get what you came for."

She handed him the hot glass. He looked from it to Helen to the girl, dumbfounded. The girl smiled at him as if to agree with Helen. There was no longer fright in her eyes, only stupefaction. She slid out from the cabinet, still in full, gaudy costume, and spread herself like a wounded bird on Dorian's lap.

"Prince Charming," she murmured. "Are you going to make sweet love to me now?" She rustled around in a daze. "I'm sorry to tell you I am not a virgin." Her eyes twinkled with sleazy secrets. Dorian took a gulp of the absinthe and waited as his senses muddled into a new keenness.

Before he knew it, he had finished the glass and Helen was back at the table refilling it.

"Will you . . ." began the girl in a slur. "Finish untying me?" She laughed and her eyes rolled back in her head.

Dorian was slow to register, but then understood that she wanted him to unfasten her corset. Blearily, he obliged. A heap of paper stuffing came out of her bodice—support to amplify her small breasts that now lay vulnerably before him. Dorian wondered how old the girl was, estimating that she couldn't be more than sixteen. What sort of life had she led? He touched her breasts lightly, as if they would tell him, and Sybil Vane writhed. She'd led a life of writhing.

"Prince Charming, are you going to make me your Princess . . . ?" she asked and paused to think of a title for herself. Unable to invent one, she giggled. "Your Princess Charming?" she said and laughed maniacally. She had teeth missing in the back of her mouth.

Helen stepped in and deftly undid the girl's petticoats, bringing them to a rustling halt against her ankles. She ran her fingers up the girl's legs. Sybil giggled squeamishly.

"That tickles!" she cried.

Dorian felt he had nodded off for a moment— absconded with a beautiful dream in which a harp was playing in mellifluous splendor and Rosemary, her sweet body lain out before him, was quivering at his touch. He snapped back into reality and saw his hands still on the slight breasts of the young but used actress. Helen was head deep in the girl's knickers.

Sybil Vane moaned contentedly, her eyes still cast in a fantasy on Dorian's. She brought her hand to his face as if to touch stained glass, a look of worship filling her eyes.

"My prince," she said, flinching as Helen's tongue darted into her. "My beautiful prince, won't you kiss me?"

And so he did, rubbing her breasts. With a tongue between either of her lips, the girl cooed and wiggled.

Together, Dorian and Helen were coaxing her into exultation. It was a kind of erotic choreography, and soon they traded places. Helen was perched at the girl's breasts, sucking her nipples, and Dorian was between her legs, rousing her with his fingers.

"Yes, my Prince," she crooned. "Come inside me now."

The absinthe and the opium and the gin were all simmering in Dorian's veins, blurring his senses, connecting them to each other and to everything around him. Sight, sound, smell, touch—it was all melting into one evanescent channel. And then there was his cock, which was taking it all in, hard as iron.

As he mounted Sybil, Helen moved aside. She sat on the floor beside them, watching as Dorian entered Sybil, relishing in the girl's cry of completeness when he pushed his cock into her and began to thrust. She was not as tight as he'd have liked, but he still felt a gentle bursting at her thick seams.

"Oh!" screamed Sybil. "Yes! My Prince!"

Dorian and Helen locked eyes, and she started rubbing herself in a fury, moaning and trembling as she brought herself to a near-instantaneous orgasm. Her face was smeared with the girl's furtive juices, and she had a drunken smile on her face. Dorian continued to thrust into the girl, feeling he could go on forever without coming. The girl's pussy tightened with each of his thrusts and he felt she was on the brink of coming. He went on thrusting, holding her hips as they gyrated and went into a flurry of spasms.

"Ah!"

The girl came in a fast flicker and flung her arms back in surrender as she subsided, panting.

Dorian felt nowhere near close to his conclusion, but went on drilling into her. He could go on forever if he must, but must he? Something was wrong.

Helen sensed it. She got up from her sunken post at the wall and came over to Dorian. She crouched down beside him, studying his position. The girl lay languidly beneath him.

"Hi," she said dreamily to Helen.

Helen looked at Dorian, who was furious in concentration. She clucked her tongue, assessing the situation, then went to the wardrobe where the girl had been tied up. She returned with the long yellow ribbon that had been used to hold Juliet's hair up, and then Sybil Vane's wrists.

"Get up," she instructed Dorian, putting a hand firmly on his sweaty shirt. He had only undone his pants. He pulled out of the girl, who promptly wailed.

"Oh, Prince Charming!" she cried. "How huge and perfect you are inside me!"

Helen grabbed the girl by both arms.

"You, too," she said. "Get up."

The girl rolled up drowsily. She looked around the room as if trying to remember where she was.

"Come on," said Helen, bringing the girl to the dressing table. She kicked one of its legs to see how sturdy it was, then tied the ribbon to the leg and the ribbon to the girl's wrists.

"Again?" murmured the girl.

"Nothing is the same thing twice," replied Helen.

"Oh," the girl said, looking at Dorian, confused. Helen's abstruse witticisms were lost on the poor girl.

"It's all good for your Prince Charming," said Dorian. Sybil smiled. "Yes," she said. "My Prince Charming."

As he watched Helen tighten the knot around the girl's wrists, he felt his erection grow. He was desperate to fuck the girl. Helen posed Sybil Vane on all fours, on her elbows and knees. Her ass was surprisingly large for her build. In the scant light it was luminous, the slender dark crack running between its cheeks gleaming, an ideal point of entry.

Dorian jumped up and seized the girl roughly by the arm. He mounted her and stuck his unyielding cock inside her, where he'd been before. The girl cried out, happy to be filled up again by him. He grabbed her hair, pulling her head back. He did not want to kiss her, but he did want to bite her, and he sunk his teeth into her neck with animal hunger. The girl cried out. When Dorian took his mouth away, he tasted blood.

"Do you like it, whore?" he asked, enraptured by his climaxing and not guarding his thoughts. Yes, she was a whore, and she was his to do with whatever he wanted. He plowed harder and harder into her, and when he felt himself about to come, he started hitting the girl—not just on her ass, but on her back and neck. His cock stiffened and grew closer to erupting its seed when he got the idea to hold her by the neck. How frail and small her bones were. It would take so little to break her. He went on thrusting as little choking sounds escaped her mouth. He came at last and remained in paradise for a stretch of moments, then let go of the girl and rolled over onto his back, breathless.

Sybil Vane was making the ugliest noises—gasping, coughing, and sounding like she may retch.

"Untie me!" she screamed.

Helen, who had been sitting out of view with a glass of absinthe, approached the girl and offered her the glass. The girl shook her head.

"Untie me!" she repeated, sobbing.

"I shall untie you," said Helen calmly. "But you shall drink this first." She held the glass out to the girl, who took a small sip.

"Another," ordered Helen. The girl heaved but did not retch and took another drink—this one a gulp.

Within a minute, her sobs subsided. Her head began to droop. Helen ducked under the table and untied her. As soon as the girl was free, she caved forward, falling on her face.

"Dorian!" called Helen.

Leaning against the shabby wardrobe, Dorian was feeling a stabbing headache coming on. His heart seemed to be racing at an abnormal pace—more rattling than beating—like a rodent caught in a plumbing pipe. He felt unable to move, and wondered with a quiet sob: Would his beautiful, young life come to an end in this forsaken back alley of a dressing room? How perfectly tragic he felt!

"Dorian!" Helen was shouting his name still. "Come here at once!"

"Yes," he said, or tried to say. There was a great static noise in the lines of communication between his brain and his body. The latter was not receiving messages clearly. And overwhelming need for sleep penetrated him. For a moment, he drifted off and into Rosemary's bosom, where he found a most extreme peace. He snapped awake in a fright. To lose consciousness now would be to risk losing it forever.

He was helplessly nodding off again when the ice water was dumped on his head, forcing him to wake up entirely. Helen was standing beside him with a metal pitcher, tapping her boot expectantly.

"I drugged the girl with laudanum to keep her from scrambling out into the street in hysterics getting herself either killed or arrested," said Helen in a strictly business tone. "But she's gone totally dead—oh, don't bug your eyes out, the insufferable actress breathes. But she is fast asleep on her face beneath her dressing table, and I need you to prop her up in her chair while I clear the scene."

Sopping wet, with a chill in his spine, Dorian stood up and approached the dressing table under which the girl lay in a naked heap. He dragged her out and laid her on her back. A cry of horror nearly escaped his lips, but the chain of command between mind and body was still too muddled to get the job done. Dark blue and black bruises streaked her neck, evidence of his prying fingers.

Behind him, Helen was wiping the glass they'd drunk the absinthe from.

"Put her here," she said, scooting out the wobbly chair. He hoisted the girl onto it. She groaned, her head swinging back, hanging from her neck like a rag doll. Dorian tilted her head forward and it slammed down on the table. Her face landed partially in the messy tins of makeup, setting off a small bomb of powder and rouge. Dorian and Helen coughed together.

Helen set the absinthe glass on the table and positioned Sybil Vane's limp fingers around the stem. She moved the near-empty chalice in front of it.

"Poor girl drank herself into a stupor," said Helen.

Dorian turned to her. He was wide awake, and his tiredness had turned into giddiness. He was hungry for more adventure.

"And now?" he asked.

"And now we go our separate ways," said Helen, looking exhausted. As she was leaving she turned back to Dorian. "Remember," she said, pointing at her eyes with two fingers and then at his. "Here."

Dorian stood around for a few minutes, at a loss without Helen's instructions. Then he remembered his belt, the only article of clothing he'd taken off. He found it coiled neatly on the floor beside the wardrobe where he'd dozed. Pity he hadn't thought of it when he was . . . no, he glanced back at Sybil Vane, who was snoring in her dusty tins, a sliver of drool growing tiny puddles around them. No, the girl had suffered enough.

CHAPTER IX

As the dawn was just breaking, Dorian found himself close to Covent Garden. The darkness lifted, and, flushed with faint light, the sky hollowed itself into a perfect pearl. Huge carts filled with lilies rumbled slowly down the empty street. The air was heavy with the perfume of the flowers. Their beauty was a dull comfort. He followed them into the market and watched the men unloading their wagons. A white-smocked carter offered him some cherries. He thanked him, wondered why he refused to accept any money for them, and began to eat them listlessly. They had been plucked at midnight, and the coldness of the moon had entered into them. A long line of boys carrying crates of striped tulips and yellow and red roses filed in front of him, threading their way through the huge, jade-green piles of vegetables. Crowds formed around the swinging doors of the coffeehouse in the piazza. The heavy cart-horses slipped and stamped upon the rough stones, shaking their bells and trappings. Some of the drivers were lying asleep on a pile of sacks. Pigeons ran about picking up seeds. After a little while, he hailed a hansom and drove home.

Wishing to not attract attention from any servants, Dorian entered through a side door connecting to the main dining room. Lights were still burning from three flickering jets: Thin blue petals of flame they seemed, rimmed with white fire. He turned them out and, having thrown his hat and cape on the table, his eye fell on the portrait Rosemary had painted of him. It was still propped against the mantle where they'd abandoned it in their passion. But the hasty wrapping was coming undone. His flawless face stared back at him. Only, no, it wasn't flawless. Something was off. Something was horribly off.

In the dim light that struggled through the cream-colored silk blinds, the face appeared to him to be a little changed. The expression looked different. One would have said that there was a touch of cruelty in the mouth. It was certainly strange.

He turned around and, walking to the window, drew up the blind. The bright dawn flooded the room and swept the fantastic shadows into dusky corners, where they lay shuddering. But the strange expression that he had noticed on the face of the portrait seemed to linger there—to be more intensified, even. The ardent sunlight showed him the lines of cruelty around the mouth as clearly as if he had been looking into a mirror after he had done some dreadful thing.

He winced and took up from a side table a mirror set in ivory, one of Helen's many presents to him in their weeks entangled with each other. He glanced hurriedly into its polished depths. But there was no snarling line like that warped in the red lips of his reflection. What did it mean?

He rubbed his eyes, came close to the picture, and examined it again. There were no signs of any change when he looked into the actual painting, and yet there was no doubt that the whole expression had altered. It was not a mere fancy of his own. The thing was horribly apparent.

He threw himself into a chair and began to think. There flashed across his mind what he had said in Rosemary's studio the day the picture had been finished. Yes, he remembered it perfectly. He had uttered a mad wish that he himself might remain young, and the portrait grow old; that his own beauty might be untarnished and the face on the canvas bear the burden of his passions and his sins; that the painted image might be seared with the lines of suffering and thought; and that he might keep all the delicate bloom and loveliness of his then just-conscious boyhood. Surely his wish had not been fulfilled? Such things were impossible. It seemed monstrous even to think of them. And yet, there was the picture before him, with the touch of cruelty in the mouth.

Cruelty! He had been cruel to Sybil Vane. A feeling of infinite regret came over him, as he thought of her bound in the wardrobe, sobbing like a little child. He remembered with what callousness he had watched as Helen tied her to the table. Why had he been made like that? Why had such a soul been given to him?

Less than a fortnight ago, he'd made love to Rosemary and had felt a true tenderness toward her. If only he could get himself back to that tenderness. But in all fairness, Rosemary had been terribly dramatic. He was reminded of some advice Helen had dispensed to him early in their friendship—that women lived on their emotions and when they took lovers, it was merely to have someone with whom they could have scenes.

But the picture? What was he to say of that? It held the secret of his life, and told his story. It had taught him to love his own beauty. Would it teach him to loathe his own soul? Would he ever look at it again?

No. It was an illusion wrought on the troubled senses. The horrible night that he had passed had left phantoms behind it. There had fallen upon his brain that tiny scarlet speck that makes men mad. The picture had not changed. It was folly to think so. Yet it was watching him, with its beautiful marred face and its cruel smile. Its bright hair gleamed in the early sunlight. Its gray eyes met his own with impenetrable darkness. A sense of infinite pity, not for himself, but for the painted image of himself, came over him. It had altered already and would alter more. For every sin that he committed, a stain would fleck and wreck its fairness. But he would not sin. The picture, changed or unchanged, would be to him the visible emblem of conscience.

He would not see Helen anymore—would not, at any rate, listen to those subtle poisonous theories that in Rosemary's garden had first stirred within him the passion for impossible things. He would apologize to Sybil

Vane—actually, no, that may be too risky considering the
state they had left her in. He would have to let that matter
be as it was and hope to forget it someday. He would go to
Rosemary and face the fact that he was in love with her.
Yes, it was his duty to do so. She must have suffered more
than he had in all this. Poor child! They could be happy
together. His life with her would be beautiful and pure.

Desperate to avoid the sickening glare of his portrait,
he went over to the table and wrote a passionate letter to
Rosemary, imploring her forgiveness and accusing himself of madness. This was not the first contact he'd made
with her since she'd stormed out in horror. But it was the
first time he made himself so vulnerable, and made special
effort not to condescend to her. He covered page after page
with wild words of sorrow and wilder words of pain. There
was a luxury in his self-reproach, and when he finished the
letter, he felt that he had been forgiven.

To complete the apology to himself, he resolved to hide
the painting, at least for the time being. In the corner of the
room stood yet another gift from Helen – an old screen of
gilted Spanish leather that was stamped and wrought with
a rather florid pattern. He hadn't cared for it much, but had
accepted it to be polite. It was even taller than he, mea-
suring nearly seven feet. He wondered: Had it ever before
concealed the secret of a man's life? It had lived at Helen's
house before, so it had probably concealed, at one time or
another, a man, but the secret of his life? That was doubtful.

He picked up the portrait and set it behind the screen.
As soon it was hidden, he felt romantic again and decided

on a stroll in the garden. When he stepped out on the grass, he drew a deep breath. The fresh morning air seemed to drive away all his somber worries. He thought only of Rosemary. How wonderful the whole world became to one in love! Oh, she was so shy and so gentle. There was something of a child about her.

It seemed to him that all his life had been narrowed to one perfect point of rose-colored joy. He remembered how, in his arms, as he'd plunged his cock into her, claiming her virginity, she trembled all over and shook like a white narcissus. How she flung herself over onto her stomach for him to take her as he pleased. Of course, he'd gotten carried away, but he would repair that.

"Rosemary . . ."

He repeated her name over and over again. The birds that were singing in the dew-drenched garden seemed to be telling the flowers about her.

At some point, he staggered back upstairs and into his bedroom where he collapsed on top of the bed, his heart still aflutter with a love song for Rosemary. He no longer felt he would die if he slept. No, he would live if he slept! Fatigue sunk his teeth into him, then swallowed him whole.

It was long past noon when he awoke. He rang his bell for his valet, who came in softly with a cup of tea and a pile of letters on a small tray of antique china, and drew back the olive satin curtains, with their shimmering blue lining, that hung in front of the three tall windows.

"Monsieur has slept well this morning," said Victor, smiling.

Dorian grunted and got up. He sipped some tea and turned over his mail. There was a package from Helen that had been brought by hand that morning. He hesitated for a moment, and then put it aside. The other letters he opened listlessly. They contained the usual collection of cards, invitations to dinner, tickets for private views, programs of charity concerts, and the like that are showered on fashionable young men every day.

After about ten minutes, he got up and, throwing on his elaborate silk-embroidered robe, went into his marble-floored bathroom. The cool water refreshed him after his long sleep. He felt all that he had gone through to that point was happily forgotten. A dim sense of having taken part in some strange tragedy came to him once or twice, but there was the unreality of a dream about it. As soon as he was dressed, he went downstairs to the main dining hall. The upper dining room was small and got poor light at this hour. He sat down to a light French breakfast that had been laid out for him on a small round table close to the open window. It was an exquisite day. The warm air seemed laden with spices. A bee flew in and buzzed round the blue-dragon bowl that, filled with sulfur-yellow roses, stood before him. Dorian felt perfectly happy. Then his eye fell on the screen, and he started with a shiver.

"Too cold for Monsieur?" asked Victor, refilling his teacup. "Shall I shut the window?"

Dorian shook his head. "I am not cold," he murmured, eager for Victor to leave so that he may examine the portrait alone.

Was it all true? Had the portrait really changed? Or had it been simply his own imagination that had made him see a look of evil where there had been a look of joy? Surely a painted canvas could not alter? And yet how vivid his recollection was of the whole thing! First in the dim twilight and then in the bright dawn, he had seen the touch of cruelty around the warped lips. He almost dreaded his valet leaving the room. He knew that when he was alone he would have to examine the portrait, and he was afraid of certainty. When the coffee and cigarettes had been brought and the man turned to go, he felt a wild desire to tell him to remain. As the door was closing behind him, he called him back. Victor stood, awaiting orders.

"I am not at home to anyone, Victor," he said.

The old man bowed and left.

Dorian rose from the table, lit a cigarette, and flung himself down on a luxuriously cushioned couch that stood facing the screen.

Should he check behind it? What was the use of knowing? If the thing was true, it was terrible. And if it was true, why worry about it? But then again, what if, by some fate or deadlier chance, eyes other than his spied behind and saw the horrible change? What should he do if Rosemary—not just the painter of the picture, but the woman he loved—came and asked to look at her own picture? The thing had to be examined—and at once. Anything would be better than this dreadful state of doubt. He got up and locked the front doors, as well as the one connecting to the rest of the house. At least he would be alone when he looked upon the mask of his shame. He drew the screen aside and saw himself face-to-face. It was perfectly true. The portrait had altered. As he often remembered afterward, and always with no small wonder, he found himself at first gazing at the portrait with a feeling of almost scientific interest. That such a change should have taken place was incredible to him. And yet it was a fact. Was there some subtle affinity between the chemical atoms that shaped themselves into form and color on the canvas and the soul that was within him? Could it be that what the soul thought, they realized—that what it dreamed, they made true? Or was there some other, more terrible reason? He shuddered and felt afraid, and, going back to the couch, lay there, gazing at the picture in sickened horror. One thing, however, he felt that it had done for him was make him conscious of how unjust, how cruel, he had been last night. There were opiates for remorse, drugs that could lull the moral sense to sleep. But here was a visible symbol of the degradation of sin. Here was an ever-present sign of the ruin men brought upon their souls.

Three o'clock struck, then four, then the half-hour rang its double chime, but Dorian did not stir. He was trying to gather up the scarlet threads of life and weave them into a pattern, to find his way through the labyrinth of passion through which he was wandering. He did not know what to do, or what to think.

There came a rapid knocking on the front door, and Dorian leaped up in fright. The punishment to which of his ghastly deeds awaited him? His recent sins fanned through his mind, rotating and colliding into one another like the twisting of a depraved kaleidoscope.

Victor's padded shoes came shuffling down the hall toward the door. Dorian thought to hide, but where and from what? He thought of Sybil Vane, her neck blackened by his greedy hands. She wore the very fingerprints of his corruption. What if she had not awoken? Far more frightening than the idea of a haunted portrait soaking up his evil was the idea of the police after him. They would not work so subtly or poetically. They'd put him away for murder.

The knocking continued and grew louder. He secured the portrait behind the screen and passed into the library, where he paced the room in tight, paranoid circles as Victor answered the door.

In rolled Helen in bright garbs, chattering away. Dorian was frozen beside the screen.

"And so I am sorry I am late, my dear," she went on. "I went to look after a piece of old brocade in Wardour Street and had to bargain for hours for it. Nowadays, people know the price of everything and the value of nothing."

She looked like a bird of paradise that had been out all night in the rain. Then, as she moved past Dorian, she just looked like a bird, flitting around the room in a bright chartreuse dress, her hair pulled back in a tight bun, her

Roman nose like a beak. Her perfume cast a false flowery aura on everything. Lighting a cigarette, she flung herself down on the sofa in front of him. What would he do now? Throw her back onto the street? No, it was better to speak with her calmly and explain to her the new life he was going to lead, to quarrel with her if it became necessary to quarrel, to part if parting was inevitable.

"How upset you look" she said, looking at Dorian at last, while sucking on her cigarette. "Have you been crying? Dear Dorian, you must not get so invested in emotions. You'll go bankrupt!"

Seeing her again, after hours of solitude and a brief vortex of sleep, he felt powerfully contrite. There was a need to talk in him he hadn't known since boyhood, when at confession he had sobbed of his misbehavior.

"I was brutal, Helen, perfectly brutal," he said.

"Is this about Sybil Vane?"

"Yes, Helen," he said, sitting down across from her. "This is about Sybil Vane. And the other women whom I've made my submissive slaves so as to indulge my dark fancies. But I think that most of all, this is about Rosemary."

"Ah, of course it is. Precious Rosemary. Her maidenhead shattered! Listen, my boy, you did the girl a favor."

Helen sunk into the cushions and, clamping her cigarette between her freshly painted lips, pulled off her long pearl-white gloves.

"Helen, I don't want to be cruel to Rosemary anymore. I love her and I must make her love me again. She is divine beyond all living things. She spiritualizes me. My God,

Helen, how I worship her! She is a genius and yet has no pretentious notion of her powers. She is pure and generous and loving. She could give me everything."

Helen was silent, folding and unfolding her gloves in her lap. Dorian searched her face for anger or sadness, but there was nothing to be found. Then she settled into a wicked smile.

"Yes, Rosemary is very generous. People are very fond of giving away what they need most themselves. It is what I call the depth of generosity."

"Ah! Helen, your views terrify me."

"Thank you."

Dorian couldn't help but laugh.

"You are incorrigible, Helen! It is impossible to be angry with you, but angry or not, I love Rosemary. I want to place her on a pedestal of gold and to see the world worship the woman who is mine. What is marriage? An irrevocable vow. You mock it for that. Ah! Don't mock. It is an irrevocable vow that I want to take. Her trust makes me faithful, her belief makes me good. When I am with her, I regret all that you have taught me. I become different from what you have known me to be. I am changed, and the mere touch of Rosemary Hall's hand makes me forget you and all your wrong, fascinating, poisonous, delightful theories."

"And those are . . . ?" asked Helen.

"Oh, your theories about life, your theories about love, your theories about pleasure. All your theories, in fact, Helen."

"Pleasure is the only thing worth having a theory about," she said. "But I am afraid I cannot claim my theory as my own. It belongs to Nature, not to me. Pleasure is Nature's test, her sign of approval. When we are happy, we are always good, but when we are good, we are not always happy."

"Ah! But what do you mean by good?" cried Dorian. He stood up and resumed pacing with little self-awareness.

"To be good is to be in harmony with one's self," Helen replied. "Discord is to be forced to be in harmony with others. One's own life—that is the important thing. As for the lives of one's neighbors, if one wishes to be a prig or a Puritan, one can flaunt one's moral views about them, but they are not one's concern. Besides, individualism has really the higher aim. Modern morality consists in accepting the standard of one's age. I consider that for any man of culture to accept the standard of his age is a form of the grossest immorality."

"But, surely, if one lives merely for one's self, Helen, one pays a terrible price for doing so?" asked Dorian. He was desperate for her spoiled wisdom.

"Yes, we are overcharged for everything nowadays. I should fancy that the real tragedy of the poor is that they can afford nothing but self-denial. Beautiful sins, like beautiful things, are the privilege of the rich."

Ah, she was so good at getting him intrigued. He felt he could stay here all day picking apart philosophical quandaries, holding ideas up in the light, discovering them to be as transparent as an insect's wings.

"One has to pay in other ways but money," said Dorian.

"Oh! Yes, one pays in remorse, in suffering, in . . . well, in the consciousness of degradation," said Helen, shrugging. "My dear fellow, medieval art is charming, but medieval emotions are out of date. Believe me, no civilized man ever regrets a pleasure, and no uncivilized man ever knows what a pleasure is. Now love away, dear Dorian, but I know you know what pleasure is," said Helen, raising her eyebrow suggestively.

Memories of their sexual escapades rushed into his mind. He blinked them away, or as away as he could. Nowadays in his consciousness, there seemed always to be a breast here and an erection there. Sexual imagery had become a part of his mind's luxurious décor.

"Yes, I know what pleasure is," he said. "But there are fleeting pleasures and then there are lasting ones. When you adore someone as I adore Rosemary, the pleasure is much deeper, much more real feeling than just . . ." he stopped talking. It still felt improper to say the word "fucking" to a woman. But to call it lovemaking would be wrong. They had never made love. And last night's incidents backstage? Why, that was just cruelty.

"Oh, yes, to adore. It is certainly better than being adored," said Helen, and laughed dryly. "Being adored is a nuisance. Rosemary treats you just as humanity treats its gods. She worships you."

"You must admit, Helen, that women give to men the very gold of their lives," said Dorian.

"Possibly," she sighed, "But I'm still pretty golden and I don't see old Lord Wotton anywhere, do you? Anyway, back to this issue of fleeting and lasting pleasures, I'm afraid I disagree with you. Right now, you are bewitched. You have no concept of time. Love is life, Dorian, and time dries up all life. Only the life of love dies much sooner than that of flesh. That is why marriage is so depressing. Its victims have no idea that what they are signing up for as eternity is merely a season, a brief springtime that will freeze up and starve like every other."

"Helen, you are dreadful! I don't know why I like you so much."

"You will always like me, Dorian," she said. Her eyes were lit with an exquisite fire. There was a radiance about her. Her parted lips were smiling over some secret of their own. "Because I will always tell you the truth." She hesitated. "Why did you not open the package I had delivered to you?"

"I apologize," he said. "I shall do so later."

"You may want to open it before you go," she said. "It contains an important truth that, based on what I am hearing, is rather pressing."

Dorian shook his head. Helen was getting into his head again, and he would not have it, not when his mind was made up for Rosemary.

"Helen, this behavior we've been engaging in, it was perhaps, in some blasphemous way, necessary to me. It awakened my soul. But my soul is one that wants to do good. It wants to be with Rosemary, for she is the pinnacle of all that is good. I must insist that you go now as I have to go find my love and repent."

He did not wait for her to respond, and fled his own home as if it were infested with vermin. When he got into the warm air, he believed he was free to love the woman he wanted and for his soul to do good. His was a beautiful existence. Even the portrait must be smiling for him.

CHAPTER X

Rosemary badly wanted Dorian's cock inside her—more badly than ever before. How ever had she taken it for granted, so much so that she'd been refusing it all these weeks? She lay in a thin chemise, turning on top of her ruffled bed. She had just read his letter for the sixth time before tossing it in the air so that its pages could land at random all over her—his apologies and promises to be read by her needy flesh. She closed her eyes and willed a dream of him.

After she'd stormed out of his house, her virginity dripping its scarlet loss down her stockings, she stumbled toward home in a kind of vertigo, still dizzied from the heights she'd fallen from—heights of unthinkable pleasure, and unbearable pain. Halfway to her house, she became queasy and ducked into a hansom. She blurted her address in a sob, then lay on her side to avoid the fire that was burning along her bottom. Her crotch felt mutilated and she dreaded whatever inspection she was bound to give it in her lonely insomnia later that night. Once home, she lay in bed for a day, getting up only to relieve herself—acts that made her cry out and relive the wreckage her love had dealt her all over again.

She vowed never to see Dorian Gray again.

The days that followed were the worst she could remember. She received a pile of letters from her father that she returned unopened. Then the letters from Dorian started popping up, frenzied notes that she opened slowly, all of them disappointing her. He explained that what he had been showing her, when he spanked and strangled her (though he used the neologisms "love-smacked" and "life-clutched"), he had been performing age-old moves of love that couples had shared throughout time. He insisted she was too naïve to understand, that in time she would learn. He apologized for giving her too much too soon.

But this latest letter was different. His handwriting was a frenzied sprint across the pages, troubling itself to keep within the margins. He assured her that he had never wished to harm her and that he, too, had been shaken by his violence. He wrote of his mother, a beautiful blue-eyed Englishwoman with chestnut hair, much like hers. Rosemary was moved to learn that they had both lost their mother as infants, that he carried around in that magnificent soul of his a sorrow much like hers. He wrote that he was telling her something he had never told anyone: that deep down, he loathed his mother for leaving him, that part of him just wanted to hurt her for the pain she'd caused him with her absence—voluntary or not. Rosemary bore such an uncanny resemblance to this exquisite woman upon whom he'd built a life of missing, Dorian wrote, that she had been fated—just that once—to take Mother Gray's beatings.

And he told her he loved her.

"I love you, I love you. My Rosemary. You're my life."

And he asked her to marry him.

"Marry me, marry me. My Rosemary. Be my wife."

Oh, the poetry! She kicked her legs and squealed. *Mrs. Dorian Gray!* She leaped up before the dressing mirror and did a pirouette, then curtsied to herself, imagining she was at a lavish ball where she and Dorian were the most talked-about guests, the most anticipated.

"Ah, yes, the name is Lady Dorian Gray," said Rosemary to her reflection, extending a hand to the glass. "Thank you, ah, you look lovely, too! Yes, it's been a splendid spring." She patted her stomach and gave a bashful smile. "Oh, yes, this gown doesn't hide a thing, does it? The child is due in August!"

Yes, she would see him. After all, could anything be worse than a life apart from Dorian Gray? So he needed to hit his mother every now and again, and she happened to look like her and was thus destined for those blows. What of it? Sex, she was learning all too quickly, was terribly complicated, and she was no saint either. She'd let him have her when he wasn't even courting her. Besides, he'd promised that he would never hit her again, and she believed him. Oh, with all her heart she believed him.

But she would have to wait to see him. She lifted her chemise and grimaced at the bulky diaper she wore. The monthly occurrence of bleeding from her womb was upon her. No man would want her in this condition. And she well knew what could happen to women who became upset by a man during this time. They could go mad. Gushing blood and prone to hysteria . . . no, she would have to wait to see her love, her husband, the father of her unconceived child. They would have many children, she would insist upon that. Any child with a drop of Dorian Gray in him or her would be in terrific luck, but Rosemary was not so bad herself. She appraised herself approvingly in the mirror. Yes, with her chestnut hair and his hooded gray eyes . . . oh, they would be such a beautiful family!

She returned to her bed. It was the middle of a gentle summer day, but it was mandatory in her condition that she remain in bed until the blood-letting was over. She mustn't get too excited either. Peace and quiet—that was what was prescribed for this monthly malady.

As she was dozing off, her butler tapped on her door.

"Yes?" she said, covering herself up. "You may enter."

Parker peeped in. He seemed to know of what Rosemary suffered at this time and regarded her with trepidation, scarcely making eye contact with her and always keeping his gloves on.

"Miss Hall, I have Mr. Dorian Gray at the door. Shall I send him away again?"

Oh, dear. This was a dilemma. If she sent him away, he would likely interpret that as another rejection. She felt that she may be running out of rejections. Dorian Gray was a gorgeous young man with all of England—and probably America, too, if he so chose it—at his fingertips.

How long would he wait around for a painter who was not getting any younger and who was, in fact, two years older than him? If she didn't accept him now, she could lose him forever.

"No, Parker, send him in, please."

"To the sitting room?" asked Parker.

Ah, yes, it would be inappropriate to have him come in here. Ah, yes, this bleeding womb was causing some crazed thoughts indeed!

"The sitting room, thank you," she said. Parker bowed and left, giving the knob an extra turn to be sure the door was securely shut.

Rosemary scrambled out of bed and ran to her wardrobe. *Easy!* She felt a warm glob of blood drop out of her.

She chose a royal blue satin gown—a gift from her father last Christmas—that she had been saving for a special event. She had fantasized that she would wear it on a date with Dorian to the theater, particularly to a performance of *Romeo & Juliet*, her favorite play. Oh, back then, just the thought of leaving her painting studio with him seemed an impossible thing. What a fairy tale it all was! Rosemary Hall, the shy painter who had banished herself to a lone life of art, would marry a wealthy and beautiful man, the very man of her, as it turned out, very real dreams.

When she emerged from her bedroom, she felt as if she were in the future, and she was coming out to meet her husband and off they would go into a night of enchantment. If only she didn't have this cumbrous swaddling around her bottom. She could hear it rustling under her petticoats. ·

Dorian was sitting at the piano. How many times she had come to greet him there! And all to lead to this moment: when she would promise to never leave him again.

"Dorian," she said.

As he turned to look at her, his mouth dropped. She felt him taking in her beauty, becoming more pleased with the choice to make her his wife when he could have any woman in England. And, Rosemary reminded herself, probably America, if he liked. The thought of American women gave her a quick pinch of anxiety. They would swarm all over him! She remembered something Helen had said when Rosemary remarked how true it was that all American women were beautiful.

"They only behave as if they were beautiful. It is the secret of their charm."

Rosemary had a heavy feeling in her chest that no matter where she was in life, no matter how far from Helen Wotton she got herself—and Dorian—that cold voice would always be with her, chucking its cruel insights at her every experience.

"Rosemary Hall," Dorian said, and stood to bow. She held out her hand, which he clutched to his mouth in a flurry of soft kisses that roused her. But she couldn't help but wonder where on Helen that mouth had been. Would she ever forgive him for his sins with her? She did not know to what extent they had been involved, but she felt they were more involved than she could handle, should ever the details be relayed to her. In his letter, Dorian said he'd been spellbound by Helen, engrossed in her wicked wisdoms. The spell was broken, he wrote, and he'd escaped her with his conscience intact.

Dorian pulled her to him, and thoughts of Helen drifted away. He held her close, and she nuzzled her nose in his neck, inhaling his soapy, musky scent. *Dorian, Dorian, Dorian.* That was the name of the man who had saved her life. She had not even known she was dying, going along her lone days, devoted to her paintings. *Paintings!* It seemed ridiculous now, that she had dedicated herself to the making of illusions, when what was real in the world was standing right before her. Perhaps all along she had just been afraid to commit herself to something mortal.

"Thank you for seeing me," he whispered.

"Oh, Dorian," She pulled back to look at him. His eyes were glowing as they took her in with a deep thirst. She had never seen such a beautiful face. She knew its every angle and shadow. She touched his cheekbones, then moved her fingers through his hair. He bowed his head submissively. She was transfigured with joy. An ecstasy of happiness dominated her. She stood on her toes to kiss him. He returned her kiss with hunger. He took her neck between his hands delicately, then ran his fingers down along her slender collarbone, grazing the tops of her breasts. She shuddered in arousal.

"You have forgiven me?" asked Dorian, as his fingers crept into cleavage.

"Yes," she answered. Her breasts were particularly full and sensitive, given her womb's ailment. When he touched them, every nerve within rang out.

"You will be my wife?" he asked, giving one breast a good squeeze. She bit her lip to suppress a cry.

"Yes," she said.

He turned her chin up in his hand and kissed her again, then brought his hands back down to her breasts, rubbing them as his tongue caressed hers into motion. He held her against him and she pushed her midsection into him. Just one touch on her burning vagina and she would be free. It ached with a needy life of its own.

"We can go into your bedroom?" asked Dorian.

Rosemary felt the tickling climb start as she rubbed herself against his leg.

"Yes," she said, her breath shortening.

As they passed into the bedroom, Rosemary saw Parker hurriedly turn away from them, a look of horror on his face.

In the bedroom, Dorian leaped onto the bed and held his hands out to her.

"My beautiful wife," he said, bringing her onto his lap and kissing her. "How I feared I'd lost you."

As he kissed her, his hands went delving through her skirts. *Oh, yes.* Rosemary felt she was a purring cat, coddled into total submission by her master's powerful hand. *He will put his hand there and soothe this burning ache.* But then she remembered her diaper and her female disorder and scrambled out of his arms, clambering to the opposite corner of the bed.

"Rosemary, have I—?" Dorian looked at his hands as if they'd inflicted some cruelty.

"No," she said, and came over to him on her knees. She stroked his shoulder, then held her arms around her. She needed to not touch him and just let her desire subside.

"No, it's all very nice," she said.

"Well, what is the matter, my dear?" he asked.

"It's me," she said. "I am ill and cannot make love."

"Ill?" said Dorian, alarmed. He touched her forehead with the back of his hand. "You are a bit warm," he said, leaning in to kiss her once more.

"No," she pulled back. "I'm sorry, but I should not even be out of bed."

"We needn't get out of bed!" Dorian assured her, pulling the covers down to let himself in.

"No, Dorian, I need to be in bed by myself and rest. I only greeted you so that you would know that I love you as you love me, and I accept your apology and your proposal. Also, in regards to what you ask in the letter: Of course I will wait for your uncle to give you your mother's engagement ring. There is no rush in that. I am yours regardless."

She held up her left hand, turning it around before him to show her unadorned fingers. He grasped her hand and kissed it with his eyes searing hers.

"I have thought of nothing but making love to you," he said. "If you are too tired, may I please just lick your secret spot?"

Rosemary felt her face turning red, and the dull ache between her thighs loudened to a sharp urge. A low moan broke from her. She wanted nothing more.

"Oh, Dorian!" she cried, and flung her arms around his neck. She rested her face against his shoulder. How small she was in comparison to him. How safe he would keep her.

"What is it, dear?"

"I am bleeding from my womb!" she blurted out. "I am one of the accursed women who suffers this condition. It sickens no one more than me, and I am so sorry that I am prone to this ailment." She bowed her head. "It happens every month. Yes, every month indeed! Typically around the 5th. But it lasts no longer than through the 13th."

She covered her face with her hands, peering at him through the slits between her fingers.

"It's all right," said Dorian, lowering her hands and holding them in his, where they were as if devoured, so miniature were they in comparison.

"I do not love you any less for this. And it is quite normal, my dear. Though I agree that eight days is a rather drawn-out vigil."

"It is?" she asked. Oh, she'd known there was something wrong with her. Dorian was just being kind.

"Yes," he said. He kissed her chastely on top of her head. "But we will work with it," he said, adding, "But it is true that you must be treated with great care during this ghastly time, and make as little exertion as possible. I have been dreaming of licking you, of savoring your sweet taste in my mouth, but to drive you to such ecstasies would be dangerous," he said. He looked at her in all seriousness, and nodded as if to be sure she was comprehending him. She nodded back in agreement, though she did not really know what she was agreeing to. He seemed to know a great deal about how a woman's body functioned in this time. She would submit to his wisdom, but, ah, what a shameful mess this all was.

"This is not the end of days, my dear flower," he said. "You must relax, but here—" He led her hand down to his crotch. His cock swelled hugely against his pants.

"You can still feel my desire for you," he said.

Rosemary felt around the erect area that was apparently his desire for her. She was unsure what she was supposed to do that would not risk her own perilous arousal. She was also just unsure in general. She knew she had to keep the cock hard, but felt clumsy and shy and worried she'd make it soft. She was grateful when Dorian spoke up and took control.

"You may unbutton the pants," he said. His voice was not exactly stern, but neither was it brimming with love and understanding. His tone was rather clinical, like he was guiding a novice in minor surgery.

Rosemary complied, gasping as his monumental cock emerged. She stroked it like he had shown her the first time. His eyelids fluttered, and she rubbed more vigorously with both hands. She went on doing this for what felt like a long time, her own desire creaming her diaper, and the aching want there growing to a pounding need. How she wanted to slip him inside of her and ram her against her hemlock headboard with its sweet stenciling of faeries and horses. But she was frightened, too, remembering the monster he'd become the last time he'd made love to her.

She kept stroking him until he abruptly removed her hands.

"Lie down," he told her.

Oh, dear, was he going to take her in this state? She felt powerless to stop him, she was so desperate to have him between her legs and heaving on top of her. She fell back on the bed, then sprang back up, remembering she would have to undo her swaddling and douche herself in the toilet.

"Where are you going?" asked Dorian.

She bit her lip.

"I must clean myself," she said. Curiously, she felt she ought to use the word "master."

"There's no need for that," said Dorian, patting the bed where she was to lie.

"But—" she started, and sat back on the bed.

"Rosemary," he said, kissing her neck up to her ears, sucking lightly on her earlobe. The heat of his tongue traveled straight down through her. Her legs twitched.

"I am not going to make love to you here," he said, his fingers passing down to her skirts. He drew his fingers back up to her face, circling her mouth. "I am going to make love to you here," he said. Rosemary's eyes bulged. She held her mouth shut. Then she let go of it and tried to smile as if all were well. Then she held it again. Resuming control, Dorian took both her hands in his.

"It's quite a normal act," he said. "When a woman is in your vile condition, one that she—that you—cannot help, for it is nature's cruel course, then one must become creative."

He stood and lifted her up—she felt like a little doll in his arms—and set her against her headboard, bringing a pillow to bolster her lower back. His cock was still hard and high in the air. Rosemary regarded it with a nervous gnash of teeth. Her teeth! Wouldn't they get in the way of all this? She remembered how he'd strangled her the first time. Would this not be another form of asphyxiation? If she could hardly manage his cock in her hands, how was she to fit it in her mouth? *Tell him you can't do it*, she thought. *It's too much.* But to think such words would have to be enough. She could not disappoint him. He loved her. There was so much at stake. If she couldn't please him during this unclean time, then what hope was there for their future? He was right, too. Eight days a month was a long time, and no husband should have to wait in abstinence. That was how they ended up at brothels.

"If you sit up on your knees, that may be more comfortable for you," Dorian said, fluffing a pillow and setting it on the bed. He tapped it and she rose up and placed her knees on it. She looked at him for further instruction.

"Oh, Rosemary, you look so beautiful right now," he said, touching her cheek. "I hope you know it will give me great pleasure to watch you while you do this. If it gets to be too much, just signal with your hand, but please don't stop abruptly, as that can be painful for me. And also," he grabbed her hand and placed it on his ball sack, "keep massaging these like you did before. You can pull harder than that, remember?"

"Yes." Oh, how she wanted to please him. She crouched down and, taking what felt to be the deepest breath of her life, faced his cock. She had not been this close to it before. It was longer than her head and as wide as her smile. She gave a small lick, and felt like a kitten in a tree.

"Put it into your mouth, slowly," he said. "Don't be afraid."

Rosemary nodded, and accidentally banged her head against his cock. They both let out an "Argh!"

Once it was in her mouth, she felt it could be reckoned with.

"Deeper," he said. "Put it in as far as it will go."

Goodness, was it only halfway in? Holding his balls with one hand, she used her other hand to guide the rest— or most of the rest—of his cock in. It was hot and salty. A large vein protruded down the base of the shaft. She ran her tongue along it, and Dorian quivered in excitement.

"Yes," he said. "Oh, Rosemary."

He put his hands on her head and rocked her back and forth, his cock feeling parts of her throat that had never been touched by flesh. She kept her lips clamped around her teeth. Saliva spilled out the sides of her mouth, helping his cock to slide in and out of her mouth with more ease. At one point, she gagged—a hideous froggy sound. She went on more vigorously, pulling on his balls all the while, using the central vein as a compass for her tongue.

Her own arousal was still calling attention to itself, bubbling beneath her petticoats, but she was resigned to getting this present job done. She kept on until she felt his cock spasm as it had when he had been about to unload his seed inside her. He stilled her head with his hands. She moved him only with her fingers.

"Ah!" he cried, and cried again. It was on the third cry that a river gushed into her mouth, filling her cheeks. She crawled off him and spat over the edge of the bed.

Dorian lay back, regaining his breath. He felt dumbly around for Rosemary, and finding her hand, clutched it to his heart.

"My dear, that was very enjoyable," he said. "You will become very good at it, in time, I think. We have eight days to practice."

Rosemary drew closer to him, wrapping his arm around her.

"Did I not do everything right?" she asked, glancing at the puddle of sperm on the ground. *Wasn't that proof of success?*

"Oh, my darling," he said, kissing her hand. "It was fine. But there were a couple moments when I felt your teeth, which you can imagine is excruciating, for the male organ is quite sensitive. Also, toward the end, you must jerk rapidly with your hand but desist using your mouth."

Rosemary rolled away from him and sighed. There was something she had to say to Dorian, but she didn't know what. The whole process had resulted in dissatisfaction. She wanted to please him more than anything, and had believed she had, yet here he was critiquing her while her own nether parts burned with ungodly passion.

She didn't want to be in bed any longer, but recalling everyone's orders, she snuggled up against Dorian and closed her eyes. He was snoring faintly.

Well, it would only be eight days a month. And at least he hadn't hit or strangled her. Life had much improved since that morning when she'd worried she'd be alone forever. She looked at her hand where Dorian's mother's ring would soon rest in promise. She thought of her own mother. The woman had not loved her father, but she had loved someone else—so much so that she had left a family behind. Rosemary hated her for that, but she also understood her. As she looked on at the sleeping Dorian Gray, still quietly snoring (an endearingly humanlike god), she wondered what she would abandon for him. She was so much luckier than her mother. To say *everything* didn't mean much.

CHAPTER XI

Dorian had asked to see her again in the days following his initial visit, but she had declined his company, insisting she was too fatigued. Her erotic craving for him was too intense to bear another unrequited act, however right a thing it was to do.

By the eighth morning of her menstruation, all bleeding had ceased. The long bed rest had made her feel weak and atrophied. She forced herself to eat a hearty breakfast, the first full meal she'd had in a week. Parker set the day's mail before her. On the top lay a hand-delivered note from Dorian, announcing that he was sending a hansom for her at eleven o'clock, and that he would expect her unclothed and in his bed by noon. She slurped up the remainders of her breakfast and hurried to bathe and dress.

As she sat in the carriage, she contemplated a worrisome thought that had begun to fester and grow in the last few days. Granted, she had been half insane with feminine bloodshed and so in no place of logic or judgment, but she felt unable to shake it off. The night before, tired from sleeping all day but unable to sleep any longer, she had consulted a book Helen had given her some time ago called *The Passions of Alphonse Gris.* It was Helen's favorite work of literature, an obscure, wretched novel that Rosemary hardly had the stomach to skim through, let alone bury herself in as Helen had. But she recalled the protagonist, the young Alphonse, had been fond of feasting upon women in a most lurid fashion. One after the other he scarfed them down and left them for near-dead. In one passage so vivid Rosemary had to squint to see straight after, the young Alphonse had taken a woman by way of her bottom—an unthinkable act—and strangled her while he mounted her, ripping tendrils of her hair out with his occasionally free hand. When Alphonse was done with her, she was grappling for life. That was only in the second chapter.

Was Dorian Gray an Alphonse Gris of sorts?

No, he was beautiful—inside and out. He'd been so elegant and innocent when she painted him. Yet since then, there was much to conflict with her original impressions of him. She recalled how when he'd made love to her, his hands had dug into her neck, like a bear's claw. Her bottom had been bruised from the blows he'd dealt. And then there was the letter begging for forgiveness, claiming madness and vowing to never cross such boundaries again. The words had sprinted from one end of the page to the other as if they were running away from him, as if he could not hold onto them.

She would have to talk this through with him. The carriage deposited her on the stone path to his house, and she walked it with a delighted sense of her own bravery and nodded to the golden poppies as if to assure them of their beauty and her own.

Victor opened the door for her and bowed simply, then plodded back down the hall into one of the many expansive, dark rooms. The house got so little sunlight, Rosemary noted. She would have to do something about that if she were expected to live there. Ah, to live with Dorian Gray! It was all such a fairy tale come true!

Before heading up the stairs she peered into the main dining hall to see if he'd hung her painting up as promised. He had not—but he had put it somewhere as it was no longer against the mantle. Where might he have placed it?

As she entered his bedroom and saw the heavy curtains blocking the windows, and the enormous bed in the center of the room, looking so pristine and tidy in its tightly tucked brocade coverlet, she felt sickened by the memory of what had taken place there last time. Surely, there had been pleasure—unbelievable pleasure—but then there had been brutality, too. She had cried out for him to stop, but he had just gone on practically murdering her. It was difficult to swallow when she thought of how he'd held her neck. Had he wanted her dead, for even a split second? No, of course not. She'd seen his soul, and it was bereft of homicidal intentions. Why, it was as beautiful as his face! What had occurred was just as he'd said; he'd gotten carried away, and as the sexually experienced probably all knew, such violence was part of the advanced lovemaking process. Perhaps, in time, she would learn to enjoy it all.

She undressed in the corner of the room, by the mirror but out of its view, and crept into the bed, taking up but one-fourth of it and sealing herself in like a candy in a wrapper. Victor was likely informing Dorian of her arrival. She could expect him to come in at any moment. Would he knock or just walk in? Was she already his, or still something to be asked for? She felt she needed to prepare herself for something, yet she couldn't think of what. His instructions had been simple. All she had to do was lie there and wait, and soon he would be on top of and inside her. Yet she felt uncomfortable, her thoughts itching and distracting her.

He knocked, but he did not wait for her to answer, and when he saw her in bed, there was no question in his eyes. He was dressed simply in a shirt and pants, with no tie, no belt, and no shoes. He looked as if he'd been lounging about all morning. This was backstage Dorian Gray. This is what she would come to know and love until death took her away from everything. God willing that death was not at his hands.

She murmured hello, her voice squeaky. Why was she so nervous? He sat beside her on the bed, his gray eyes steely on hers. As he took her hands in his, she felt chills of anticipation down her neck and a tingling heat between her thighs. He went to uncover her, and was on the brink of kissing her, when she started to talk. She talked in a high and fretful voice. The words from her mind were unmoored by her mouth.

"I will try and do something, Dorian, if it would please you. I—I don't think I'm cut out for the type of things you indulge in," she said.

Dorian did not back his face away, his mouth still hovering inches away from hers, but he squinted as if he was not comprehending her. She went on.

"It's not that I disapprove—not at all do I disapprove!" she said, lifting her right hand and pressing it to her heart. "But for me, it is frightening, and I wish you would tell me some other things I could do to please you. If you are truly the kind of person who needs to inflict pain in order to . . ." Rosemary cringed at the direction the sentence was going. Then she cringed at herself for cringing. Would she ever be rid of this priggish provincialism? She thought of the insidious Alphonse from the yellow book Helen had sent her. Who were these people? And Dorian's friendship with Helen . . . what had come of that? What had they been involved in together? Why was there no way to stop thinking? She should at least be able to stop talking, seeing Dorian's confused expression, but, no, she kept going.

"Well, perhaps I may never satisfy you," she said, her cheeks hot with shame. "Yet, deep down—the Dorian I painted—I don't feel he, umm, *you* are such a man."

"Shh," he said, leaning in to kiss her softly. Her lips were hungry for his and as his tongue probed for hers, her mind's chatter stilled and there was a mental silence like a cooling breeze. She crossed her legs as another fire started up between them.

But once his mouth was away from hers again, she felt it necessary to solve the matter at hand. But, oh, how to talk about these things? Who knew that sex was so complicated? And did she even know what she was talking about? She didn't think so. Other than the passage in that horrible book, she really had no clue. In one or another of the sordid monologues she made Rosemary sit through, Helen had laughed about all the boys who were too timid to spank her bottom. She'd shrugged off her husband, disparaging him for possessing only the nerve to ram his cock down the mouths of whores, but not his wife's. She said quite horrific things about Lord Wotton's penis, indeed—that it was small (she had held up her pinky finger) and curved like screw. Whenever Helen talked about sex, Rosemary did all she could to drown her out. Usually she was stooped at her easel, painting some innocuous landscape. Now she wished she'd taken notes.

Dorian pressed his finger to her mouth again.

"Rosemary, I've expressed my utmost love for you," he said. "I do not wish to hurt you. I am controlling those urges."

"Yes, I know!" cried Rosemary, as she leaped up and into his arms. She caressed his cheeks and lips, marveling at his stoic beauty. How unbelievable that he was hers! But could she give him what he wanted? Would he settle for a life of traditional lovemaking? And Helen—though she had to believe that Dorian was no longer under her spell, she knew that Helen would always be lurking in the shadows, scowling at their happiness. She would be looking for weakness in their bond, anything to separate them. But to obsess over Helen would only trouble Rosemary further, she thought. She needed to focus on her relationship with Dorian and nothing else. Yet there was something changed in Dorian that still she could not identify. Just then, she had an idea.

"My darling!" she cried. "If I could just understand you the way I understood you while I painted you. I feel certain that if I painted you again—as my lover and not just my friend—I could understand you once more, only deeper. Before, I was too shy to look at you in that light."

As she spoke, she felt warm and united with her love. It was a brilliant idea! But Dorian became cold and solitary.

"I can never sit for you again, Rosemary," he said.

He got up from the bed and went before the mirror, where he stared at himself, brooding. Rosemary rolled into a fetal position under the covers. He was being so strange! She felt she would surely die if he continued to act in this unloving way. She wasn't asking for much, was she? Really, he should be willing to do anything for her since she was here in his bed despite all that had transpired. She sniffled when she thought of how he had hurt her in the past and how he had made her suck his enormous member and then how he made her feel as if she'd done an insufficient job. After they had first made love, it had been impossible for her to sit in proper posture for three days. And here he wouldn't even sit for her at all.

"It is impossible!" he cried.

"I don't understand why you are so adamantly oppo-sed," said Rosemary. She was well aware that she was star-ting to nag at him, which was something she had never done before. She took a moment to revel in the honor: The first man she'd nagged was the gorgeous Dorian Gray! If only she had a friend to brag to about it. Oh, dear, that was another thing to be upset about: She had no friends. The one friend she'd had she'd lost because of Dorian. She would have to nag him about that later.

"Rosemary, I have my reasons. Please respect them," said Dorian.

Watching him watch himself reminded Rosemary that he was the perfect man. For a moment, she wanted only to lie down with him and have him take her again. But, no, she scolded herself—she had to hold her ground. If there was to be any future between them, she had to know why he acted as he did.

"We must talk about this," she persisted.

"I don't care to discuss it," said Dorian. "Let us change the subject or not talk at all."

They made eye contact in the mirror, and Rosemary softened. She remembered how much of a struggle it had been for him to sit still for his portrait the first time. And now she wanted to put him through a second sitting? Maybe this was all a matter of him not wanting to put up with the posture and the long hours. The first painting had been all about seduction anyway, hadn't it? Yes, and now they had each other. Why put this sacred god of a man through more suffering?

"All right, I'll let it go," said Rosemary, and then, to keep her nagging power, added, "For now."

"Thank you," said Dorian. His eyes resumed focus on themselves in the mirror. Oh, he was so beautiful! Rosemary felt giddy. She clapped her hands like a little girl.

"On another subject," she began with a childlike grin, "Well, sort of another subject, it's still somewhat the same subject—but, anyway," she batted away her annoying Rosemary-esquenes. "I have good news about the portrait!"

Dorian whipped his head around.

"What news?" he asked.

"I am going to exhibit it in Paris in the autumn!" she cried, clapping again.

Dorian's eyes narrowed. He looked as if he could strangle her. This made her shamefully wet between the legs.

"Are you proud of me?" she said, flinging the bed covers off. She lay stretched on her side like a model she'd seen in a dirty daguerreotype and put her finger in her mouth suggestively.

"Georges Petit is giving me my own show," she said in a kittenish voice. "I'm the only woman to be featured. He's going to collect all my best pictures for a special exhibition in the Rue de Sèze this coming autumn."

She crawled to the edge of the bed and held her hand out to Dorian, reaching for his pant leg. He was but a foot away, yet refused to come any closer. All tenderness had deserted his face. Oh, but wasn't he mysterious?

She sat up, feeling acutely self-conscious, and wrapped herself back in the creamy satin sheets.

"I promised him the portrait," she said, speaking plainly. "And since it will only be away a month, I should think you could easily spare it for that time."

"To exhibit it?" asked Dorian, stunned. "You want to exhibit it?"

"Yes," Rosemary said. What a perplexing man he was! "Which means I shall probably need to give it another coat of varnish, which I can take care of at once. I can do it today, even!"

"No!" cried Dorian, leaping onto the bed beside her as if to stop something from ringing—or a bomb from going off.

"What is the matter?" asked Rosemary. "If you always keep it behind a screen, you can't care much about it."

Dorian sat up and passed his hand over his forehead, where beads of perspiration had gathered.

"If you try to look at it, Rosemary, on my word of honor I will never speak to you again as long as I live," he said. "I am quite serious. I don't offer any explanation, and you are not to ask for any. But remember, if you touch that screen, everything is over between us."

Rosemary was struck into silence. She had never seen him like this before. He was actually pallid with rage. His hands were clenched, and the pupils of his eyes were like disks of gray fire. He was trembling all over.

"Dorian, you must stop this behavior, or explain yourself!" cried Rosemary. She felt as certain as ever that she
did not know the least about who Dorian Gray was. What
made her so sure then than she loved him—that he loved
her? She folded up in the sheets and, hiding her face, began
to sob quietly. Dorian rushed to her side.

"My dear child," said Dorian, embracing her. Rosemary
resisted, but he pulled her onto his lap, and she hugged
herself up in a ball. Dorian spoke to her calmly.

"You told me a month ago that you would never
exhibit it. You can't have forgotten that you assured me
most solemnly that nothing in the world would induce you
to send it to any exhibition. You told Helen exactly the
same thing."

"Ah!" cried Rosemary, crying harder at the mention of
her former friend.

"I'm sorry," whispered Dorian, rocking her in his arms.
"Helen is meaningless in this. She's got nothing to do with
it."

"But the painting is marvelous," she wailed. "I don't
understand any of this!"

And that's when it occurred to her that maybe the
painting wasn't marvelous. After all, other than herself, no
one but Dorian, Helen, and her father had seen it. And
they all had reasons to lie to her. What if Dorian was embarrassed by it and, in turn, by her, his wife-to-be?

"Dorian, do you mean to say you don't like what I
did?" she asked. "Let me look at it. I must know if it is the
best work I have ever done or not."

"Shh," said Dorian, kissing her forehead. His mood was again altered. It seemed as if he wanted to make love to her, and he fondled her breasts, continuing to hush her.

"It was your best work. . . . Now, shh . . . oh, how I must bury my head in these gorgeous breasts!"

"*Was* my best work?" Rosemary shoved her way out of his arms and got down from the bed, nearly landing on all fours. She stood up, naked, crossing her legs and pinning her hair down over her nipples.

"Has something happened to it? If there is damage, I must assess it!"

"My dear, there is no damage," he said, and held his arms out to her, smiling—an invitation to that ultimate event leering in his grin. *Don't give in*, thought Rosemary, as a droplet of lust trickled down her thighs.

"If there is no damage," she went on. "Then let us hang it above the fireplace as we planned!"

"No!" he cried and snapped back in anger. "We can't hang it above the fireplace like some cozy family."

Rosemary started back toward the door.

"Not hang it? Why? And why be so cruel? Let me see the painting."

She ran out and flew down the stairs. *Let the valet see me nude*, she thought, her fury gaining momentum as she charged through the palatial foyer. *Let them all see me!* Though as far as she knew, there was only frail, old Victor.

She sprinted into the dining hall where she'd last seen the painting. There was a stampede of steps behind her, and she was briskly whisked off the ground—abducted by her Prince Charming! She kicked her legs and spat.

"Stop," Dorian cried, shaking her. "Stop!"

She began to hyperventilate, so he slapped her a couple times on either cheek. The physical scolding eased her. She went limp in his arms. He set her down on the floor, but did not remove his hands from her shoulders, holding her firmly in place.

"Easy," he murmured. He turned her around to face him, then brought both her hands to his lips and kissed them.

"You must not see the painting," he begged. "Please, I don't wish you to. My sweet girl, let us go back into the bedroom. We will make love like angels. I will coddle you and kiss your sacred hairy parts."

His kisses, mingled with his seductive words, caused her to quiver with desire. Her vagina came alive again, throbbing, desperate for his touch. He kissed her neck and grabbed her breasts, kneading them gently until her nipples hardened. Oh, she was his no matter what! She would let him lead her back to the bedroom. As she started to get up, he pushed her back down on the plush Oriental rug, then stopped himself.

"I am so sorry!" he said, burying his head in her neck. "If you want to get up, you may, of course."

"No, this is quite fine," she said, thankful that the rug was so expensive and thus easy on the elbows. But what a paradox! Here she was, liking his enormous weight holding her down, liking being pinned helplessly beneath him. Oh, she was just a lamb! She was meant to be fallen prey to the lion. But she wasn't so sure that the lamb and lion should be doing anything outside of the bedroom. She looked around nervously. What if the valet stumbled upon them?

"You wish to stay in here?" she asked.

"Is it so terrible?" he asked. The color came back to his cheeks, and a flirtatious smile played on his lips. He gestured to the bay windows. The shutters had been pulled up. The glass gushed with sunshine.

"The light is superb," said Dorian. "I can see you."

He swept her hair behind her shoulders and leaned down to kiss and suck her breasts.

"So beautiful," he said as he raised his face to kiss her on the lips. He maneuvered his hands down to her thighs and spread them apart. Rosemary lay back into the carpet and moaned as his fingers felt through her dark, wet folds, finding her clitoris. He began to rub there slowly. *Yes*, thought Rosemary. *Oh, please don't stop.* He did stop, but only for a moment—a near-eternal moment—that saw Rosemary writhe in suspense. He replaced his massaging fingers with his full, generous mouth, and flecked her clitoris lightly with his tongue. This was too much. She cried out, and in response he began to suck and brought a finger inside her, rubbing in probing circles. She could hear his tongue lapping up her juices and it aroused her more. She dug her fingers into the carpet as she felt the orgasmic seizing begin.

Dorian came up from her legs and mounted her, easing his cock into her. Oh! She remembered the pain the first time and held her breath, preparing herself. But there was no pain this time, only a deep, grinding pleasure. She exhaled in a moan.

"Open your eyes," said Dorian. Rosemary hadn't been aware that she was keeping them shut. There was a part of her that was terribly embarrassed to be watched by him, but she opened her eyes and found in his a most moving look of adoration.

"I love you," he whispered, their eyes locked. *He loves you! Dorian Gray loves you, Rosemary Hall!* Oh, she could die of happiness. He thrust deeper into her and brought his lips to hers, lingering there. He bit ever so slightly, then stopped himself.

"It's all right," she whispered.

"No," he said.

Her climax resumed as his rhythm picked up and she knew she would come soon. Her toes curled in anticipation. She grabbed his shoulders as he dug harder into her, feeling she would shatter at any moment, if he would just keep going. She pictured his cock inside of her, activating all the tight and trembling nerves. Dorian was soon going to come, too—she could feel it in the spasming of his cock. They came together in a shared cry of relief that echoed back to them in the wide hall, where the screen stood protectively, knocked a little askew by the kicking of a foot in erotic rhapsody.

CHAPTER XII

Half awake, eyes still closed, feeling the tail end of an erotic dream crawl back into its hushed hideout, Dorian felt along the mattress for the warm body of his love. He expected to find her curled beside him, the precious doll, and he patted and patted, but there was just bare sheets, a chill running through them. He opened his eyes and shot up, panicked. He tore out of bed and into his robe.

"Rosemary!" he called. "Rosemary, darling?!"

"Monsieur?" came a rusty reply.

It was Victor, passing by with a tray.

"I was just bringing your dinner. If you had plans to go out to dine, I'm afraid it is too late."

"What o'clock is it?"

"It is nearly nine o'clock in the evening."

Dorian gasped. He never slept for more than a couple hours at a time. Even before his thrill-seeking exploits with Helen—after which he awoke sweating beads of gin and trembling from opium withdrawal—he was a troubled sleeper. Since childhood, he could not manage a night that was not clawed at by nightmares, infested with fear. He saw his mother in his dreams, under an empyrean canopy of sunlight laughing. He ran to her outstretched arms. But before he got there, a demon force lunged between them, and she was gone again forever. But Rosemary. Rosemary quelled his tormented heart and was the cooling medicine for a fever he'd always suffered.

"Victor, where is Rosemary?"

"Madam left hours ago, Monsieur," answered Victor, his face a placid mask of servility.

"Hours ago?" cried Dorian. He slammed his foot down, causing old Victor to jump. The tray wobbled in his grasp. He cried out as he nearly dropped it.

"Specifics, Victor!" cried Dorian. "At what o'clock did Miss Hall leave?"

"Why, why," Victor's voice trembled. Nearly dropping the precious tray had taken its toll on the old man, and now he was being asked to recall something he likely had not made record of in the first place. His face twisted as he tried to remember, fingering through the fog of a tired mush that was the relic of a once-competent human mind. One less thing Dorian would have to dread . . . senility.

"Did she say anything?" he asked. "Anything at all?"

Victor shook his head frantically. "No, Monsieur, not a word. She was upset. I just assumed there had been a quarrel. I did not impose myself, nor did she seek my service. She let herself out. Monsieur, she was quite upset."

"Yes, Victor," cried Dorian. "You already said so!"

"I am sorry," said Victor.

Dorian shook his head and started out of the room, pushing Victor out of his way. The old man let out a scared cry. The tray clattered to the floor, the lid taking its time as it spun down the hall.

Dorian ran downstairs and into the dining hall. Oh, he should have hidden it better! Now everything was at risk!

But the screen was just as he had left it. He peeked behind it and was assured that the painting was still there, hidden from sight. He fell down on the rug before it, where just hours ago he'd mounted his bride-to-be. He touched the screen fearfully. Oh, how he feared this portrait! He must not remove the screen ever, at least not while it lay in open sight as it did now. He quieted his movements, listening for Victor. He heard him still clearing the mess upstairs.

Had Victor seen the painting? If he had, it may not matter much, since he had not seen the original. Still, he had to keep his guard. It was likely that the portrait would continue to decay with time and sin, and Dorian could not risk Victor seeing any of that. If he did, he would have to . . . Dorian's heart thundered at the thought. Would he murder Victor? Whatever was he thinking? And if Rosemary had seen it, would he murder her?

"Ah!" he shrieked at the thought. No, he would just hide the painting more efficiently. He could not run such a risk of discovery again. It had been mad of him to have allowed the thing to remain, even for an hour, in a room to which anyone but he had access.

He went into the library where on an arm chair lay a
large, purple satin coverlet heavily embroidered with gold,
a splendid piece of late-seventeenth-century Venetian work
that his Uncle Kelso had found in a convent near Bologna.
Yes, that would serve to wrap the dreadful thing in. It had
perhaps served often as a pall for the dead. Now it was to
hide something that had a corruption of its own, worse
than the corruption of death itself—something that would
breed horrors and yet would never die. What the worm
was to the corpse, his sins would be to the painted image
on the canvas. They would mar its beauty and eat away its
grace. They would defile it and make it shameful. And yet
the thing would still live on. It would always be alive.

He shuddered and for a moment regretted that he had
not told Rosemary the true reason that he had wished to
hide the picture away. The love that he bore her—for it
really was love—was not that mere physical admiration
of beauty that is born of the senses and that dies when the
senses tire. It was such love as Michelangelo had known,
and Montaigne, and Winckelmann, and Shakespeare
himself. He was determined to have her to himself. If she
had seen the painting, how could she blame him for its
disgrace? It was a creation they had born together, and really it was probably more her fault than his, given that she
was so obsessed with him while painting it.

He took up from the chair the great purple-and-gold
texture that covered it, and, holding it in his hands, passed
back into the main hall and behind the screen. Was the
face on the canvas viler than before? It seemed to him that

it was unchanged, and yet his loathing of it was intensified. Gold hair, wintry gray eyes, and rose-red lips—they all were there. It was simply the expression that had altered and was horrible in its cruelty. But what of the revelation that he loved Rosemary? Wouldn't that appease the painting some, take some of the sinful weight off his soul? He loved her and had every intention to do right by her. He would marry her. It was not his fault that the painting was demonic. Rosemary would have to forgive him now for not letting her exhibit it.

He flung the rich pall over the picture and wondered where he could stow the painting. It came to him at once: the attic. He had not entered the place for more than four years—when he had arranged it as a study. It was a large, well-proportioned room, which had been specially set aside by his Uncle Kelso for the use of the little nephew whom, for his strange likeness to his mother, he had always hated and desired to keep at a distance.

"Victor!" called Dorian, thinking up some way to get him out of the house.

The servant came meekly out of the shadows.

"Monsieur," he said.

"It's to be terribly hot tomorrow," said Dorian. It was the only excuse he could muster. Victor was exorbitantly attentive to the garden.

"The poppies are in bad need of watering and I don't want to risk them getting singed in the heat."

"Oh, but Monsieur," started Victor, with his helpful, servile air. "I checked the garden this morning, and the

beds were still quite soiled from the storm. There is actually a bit of a mud problem, the ground is so very wet."

"Victor," said Dorian, sternly, "I have been sowing
poppies all my life. They were my mother's favorite flower!
She died when I was an infant, and so sowing poppies is
a way of remembering her. I don't want to take any risks
with them. Now, please. I appreciate your advice, but I do
not request it. Please go fill the tin and water the poppies."

"Yes, I am very sorry," said Victor. He bowed graciously
and exited. Dorian waited to hear the front doors shut,
then ran upstairs past his bedroom. Up above, at the end
of the long hallway, hung the rusty chain to the attic door.
He yanked and down came a dark, mildewed staircase.

The room was little changed. There was the huge Italian
chest, with its fantastically painted panels and its tarnished
gilt moldings in which he had so often hidden himself as
a boy. There, the satinwood book-case filled with his dog-
eared schoolbooks. On the wall behind it was hanging the
same ragged Flemish tapestry on which a faded king and
queen were playing chess in a garden, while a company of
hawkers rode by, carrying hooded birds on their gauntle-
ted wrists. How well he remembered it all! Every moment
of his lonely childhood came back to him as he looked
around. He recalled the stainless purity of his boyish life,
and it seemed horrible to him that it was here that the fatal
portrait was to be hidden away. How little he had thought,
in those simple days, of all that was in store for him!

But there was no other place in the house so secure from
prying eyes as this. Beneath its purple pall, the face painted

on the canvas could grow bestial, sodden, and unclean. What did it matter? No one could see it. He himself would not see it. Why should he watch the hideous corruption of his soul? He kept his youth—that was enough. And, besides, might not his nature grow finer, after all, since he was to devote his life to the love of another? Couldn't that love purify him? Of course, he and Rosemary would have to work out the aging predicament, given that she would likely prune up and hollow out while he remained forever in the healthy prime of youth, but they would form a strong family with sons and daughters and maybe even a few hounds. That would ease the pain of her deterioration somewhat. And modern medicine, why, it was always up to something scientifically miraculous, and there would probably be types of cures for aging, albeit none as potent as corrupting one's soul and deflecting the corruption onto a painting—but still, there would be something. There was no reason that the future should be so full of shame. Perhaps, some day, the cruel look would pass away from the scarlet, sensitive mouth, and he might show to the world his beloved's masterpiece.

He shut the attic back up, satisfied that no one would have any reason to go up there, then returned to his bedroom, where he started a letter to Rosemary, asking her to meet him the following day. He needed to know why she was angry with him. Had he not made satisfying love to her? It had been agony not to grab her neck and squeeze life from her while he was reaching what could have been an exquisite ejaculation in which he touched the Sun. He had restrained, and his orgasm had been lesser because of it—he'd merely touched a hazy horizon of an earthly sky.

As he was sealing the envelope, he noticed the brown package Helen had sent him the morning after their night of squalor at the theater. He had never opened it—indeed, forgotten all about it just as he'd tried to forget about Sybil Vane and the violent prints he'd left on her neck. He'd put it aside on the nightstand table yet here it lay in plain view on the bureau. The wrapping was ripped, revealing a thick yellow book with old, crumbling pages clinging within its flaps. Dorian grabbed it and a piece of paper fell out. It contained Helen's swift, exact handwriting. He picked it up, his hand weighted with dread. He knew that if it didn't lead back to the portrait, Rosemary's agitation led to Helen. All agitation in the life he shared with Rosemary traced back to Helen. As he read, he felt as if he'd swallowed a goblet of ice.

My Dear Dorian,

Last night was a fantastic thrill! I hope you have found your way after a long sleep into a fresh and convivial mood, and that you are not suffering any soppy repercussions of moral guilt. This book I have enclosed will help you to escape that caped madman who so boldly wrecks lives under the grim guise "Conscience." Consider this novel your Bible. It is only in fiction that fact can speak without fear.

I have been withholding some information from you, my cherished beauty, and I wholeheartedly apologize. I have promised to always tell you the truth, and I will keep that promise until my last breath (and beyond, if I do wind up in that lowly Heaven so ineptly termed Hell by the scared and sanctimonious)! The only reason I have tarried in sharing this with you is because I wanted you to have this book in your hands. . . .

Dorian, if you marry Rosemary Hall you will become wretched. As you know, I do not champion marriage, and am certain that should you marry anyone you will become unselfish, and unselfish people are colorless. But Rosemary, in particular, is not a woman to call your wife. She is, in your case and yours alone, to be called your sister.

Before your mother fled to America and met your father, she bore a daughter with an Englishman to whom she was still legally married when she ran off with Mr. Sheldon "Skip" Gray, your father. The man's name is Edmund Hall. Your Uncle Kelso, in a miserly move to both protect you from and deny you the truth (notice how often those two gestures join in one stone's throw of deceit!), created the fantasy that this daughter died during infancy. She, in fact, grew up as you did, in perfect health, just a few miles from you. . . . Now you see where this story is going. Her name was, and is, Rosemary. She paints a fine portrait.

I imagine this news is not met with elation, but I believe that in time, you will see its poetic fascinations. It often happens that the real tragedies of life occur in such an inartistic manner that they hurt us by their crude violence, their absolute incoherence, their absurd want of meaning, their entire lack of style. They affect us just as vulgarity affects us. They give us an impression of sheer brute force, and we revolt against that. Sometimes, however, a tragedy that possesses artistic elements of beauty crosses our lives. If these elements of beauty are real, the whole thing simply appeals to our sense of dramatic effect. Suddenly, we find that we are no longer the actors, but the spectators of the play. Or, rather, we are both. We watch ourselves, and the mere wonder of the spectacle enthralls us. In the present case, what is it that has really happened? Someone you loved as a wife has been revealed to be your sister. I wish that I had ever had such an experience. It would have made me in love with love for the rest of my life. Life is seldom so interesting as yours has had the fortune of being! And love nearly never is.

Remember what I once said to you: If one doesn't talk about a thing, it as if it has never happened. Telling any of this to Rosemary would create a great violence in her mind. I wonder whether the little lamb could even handle such a blow. But I leave that matter up to you.

Do not waste your tears. You will have new passions, new thoughts, new ideas.

Your Friend,

Helen

PS: We may thank my voluble Aunt Agatha for relaying this information to me.

After some time, Dorian looked up. The evening had darkened in the room. Noiselessly, and with silver feet, shadows crept in from the garden. The colors faded wearily out of things. Dorian dropped the letter. He felt it should crack and bleed when it hit the ground, but it just skimmed the lacquered wood and curled up like any leaf of paper.

CHAPTER XIII

Poor Rosemary! What a romance it had all been, and, oh, what more it could yet be had only Truth not shed its burning light, striking their love down. What would become of her? Tears came to his eyes as he remembered her childlike look when he had first sat her on his bed, the red towel under her legs. He thought of how serious and inventive she became when she was at her easel. Gone was her shy, tremulous manner as she stood an earnest disciple of a superior grace. He brushed his tears away and, with them, thoughts of Rosemary, and looked again at the picture.

He felt that the time had really come for making his choice. Or had his choice already been made? Yes, life had decided that for him—life, and his own infinite curiosity about its orgiastic elements. Eternal youth, infinite passion, pleasures subtle and secret, wild joys and wilder sins—he was to have all these things. The portrait was to bear the burden of his shame: That was all.

A feeling of pain crept over him as he thought of the desecration that was in store for the fair face on the canvas. Was it to become a monstrous and loathsome thing, to be hidden away in a locked room, to be shut out from the sunlight that had so often touched to brighter gold the waving wonder of its hair? The pity of it!

If he changed his ways and resorted to a commonplace life based on virtues that society chose for him, perhaps the portrait would escape the hideousness of sin, but the hideousness of age would be in store for it no matter what, Dorian figured. Hour by hour, week after week, it would grow old. The cheeks would become hollow and flaccid. Yellow crow's feet would creep round the fading eyes and make them horrible. The hair would lose its brightness, the mouth would gape or droop, would be foolish or gross, as the mouths of old men are. There would be the wrinkled throat, the cold, blue-veined hands, the twisted body. . . . And what if he did live the "good" life? If he took a wife— a wife he either didn't love at all or loved only in a pathetic imitation of his love for Rosemary—and forced himself into a fidelity with her? It sickened him to think of it. Surely the painting would be covered in vomit within a year or two of that scenario.

He thought of praying that the horrible bond that existed between him and the picture might be broken. It had changed in answer to a prayer; perhaps in answer to a prayer, it might stop its bewitched course. But then who, that knew anything about life, would surrender the chance of remaining always young, however fantastic that chance might be or with what fateful consequences it might be fraught? Besides, was it really under his control? Had it indeed been prayer that had produced the substitution? Might there not be some curious scientific reason for it all? If thought could exercise its influence upon a living organism, might not thought exercise an influence upon dead and inorganic things? No, without thought or conscious desire, might not things external to ourselves vibrate in unison with our moods and passions, atom calling to atom in secret love, or strange affinity?

But in the end, the reason was of no importance. Dorian would never again tempt by a prayer any terrible power. If the picture was to alter, it was to alter. That was all. Why inquire too closely into it?

A rare occurrence this was, and so maybe a rare opportunity he would be idiotic to deny himself. There could be a real philosophical pleasure in watching the portrait, to track it as it descended into his soul's secret places. He could study it over time. This portrait would be to him the most magical of mirrors. As it had revealed to him his own sexually ravenous body, so it would reveal to him his own sexually ravaged soul. And when winter came upon it, he would still be standing where summer trembles on the verge of autumn. When the blood crept from its face, and left behind a pallid mask of chalk with leaden eyes, he would keep the glamour of boyhood. Not one blossom of his loveliness would ever fade. Not one pulse of his life would ever weaken. Like a Greek god, he would be strong, and fleet, and joyous. What did it matter what happened to the colored image on the canvas? He would be safe. That was everything.

He took up the mysterious yellow book Helen had sent him. The author was listed as anonymous, and it appeared

to be as old as books themselves. The leaves hung perilously from the spine, and he had to take care, as he flung
himself into an armchair to read, not to tear them. After
a few minutes, he became absorbed. It was the strangest
book he had ever encountered. As he read, it seemed to
him that in exquisite garbs, and to the delicate sound of
flutes, the sins of the world were passing in dumb show
before him. Things that he had dimly dreamed of were
made real to him. Things of which he had never dreamed
were gradually revealed.

It was a novel that, much like life, contained no plot
and so felt all the more true. It was called *The Passions of
Alphonse Gris*. There was only one character of interest: a
young Parisian, Alphonse Gris, who spent his life trying
to realize in the nineteenth century all the passions and
modes of thought that belonged to every century except
his own, and to sum up, as it were, in himself the various
moods through which the world-spirit had ever passed,
loving for their mere artificiality those renunciations that
men have unwisely called virtue, as much as those natural
rebellions that wise men still call sin. Alphonse Gris fucked anything that walked—including a dastardly cripple
who, despite her mashed legs and thieving intentions, had
a pretty face and an exotically long tongue whose way with
the male member was unparalleled.

The style in which it was written was vivid and obscure at once. Its metaphors were as monstrous as orchids
and as subtle in color. The life of the senses was described
in the terms of mystical philosophy as well as radiant

pornography. One hardly knew at times whether one was reading the spiritual ecstasies of some medieval saint or the sensual confessions of a modern sinner. It was a poisonous book. The heavy odor of incense seemed to cling about its pages and to trouble the brain. The mere cadence of the sentences, the subtle monotony of their music, so full as they were of complex refrains and movements elaborately repeated, produced in Dorian's mind, as he passed from chapter to chapter, a form of reverie charged with lascivious energy. It was a kind of incurable sickness, the sexual intensity that fired in his loins. As he read, his cock hardened, became all bone, and more than once he had to set the book down, take to his drawer of dirty daguerreotypes, and empty his cock into a glossy cloth.

He had to keep reminding himself that its contents were only words. Words! He said the word, *words*, over and over again in his mind, feeling sanity about to topple out of his grasp. So clear and vivid and cruel words were, and what magic they withheld! They seemed to be able to give a plastic form to formless things and to have a sexual rhythm of their own.

Ah! He felt words crawling up and down his spine, tickling in his undershorts. He had to get out of his room, out of his whole house! He must smoke, and imbibe, and laugh, and dance, and, above all, he must fuck. It was decided. He would meet Helen. What good was there in hiding from his inherently bad nature? Either road he chose would be clad in sin. To stalk off into an eternal night, infinite with sexual squanders, was, in a way, less sacrilegious than marrying his sister and bearing a brood of hell-bound offspring. Yes, he would go with Helen tonight. They would eat the finest, bloodiest of chops at the St. James, and then head over to the Brandy Bell, where they would drown themselves in quartern upon quartern of the brown liquor, getting their bellies fat with false courage.

As he dressed for dinner, he watched himself in the mirror—seduced yet again by his beautiful physique. Rosemary, with her astute painter's eye, had been right. He was the living ideal of a young man. He probably need not even exercise to maintain his broad shoulders and flat, rigid stomach. And his face, the face that was so entrancing to everyone whose eyes fell upon it—why, that would never leave him. He wondered if there was a need to make it any better and examined himself from different angles. No, it was rather perfect as it was. He wetted his eyebrows with his spit to smooth them into place and rubbed his strong, smooth chin where a gruff harvest was beginning. He shaved himself in a hurry, nicking his neck in the process. It left not a trace on his skin. The portrait would bleed for him.

He was just about ready to leave, when, staring at himself, he saw someone familiar in his face—and it was not himself. By God, it was Rosemary. Yes, how had he not seen it all along? The resemblance was there in the shape of the eyes, the full lips, the flawless smile.

Oh, well, he thought.

And this was the last he thought of his love, Rosemary, for some time. She visited his dreams on occasion, but as soon as she drew her dear, succulent mouth from his, her face twisted and scowled, became disgusting. Really she resembled less him and more his other doomed sibling, the portrait.

CHAPTER XIV

For years, Dorian Gray could not free himself from the influence of the yellow book Helen Wotton had vested in him. Or perhaps it would be more accurate to say that he never sought to free himself from it.

The hero, the debauched young Alphonse Gris in whom the erotic and stoically philosophical temperaments were so strangely blended, became to Dorian a kind of prefiguring type of himself. The whole book seemed to him to contain the story of his own life, written before he had lived it. There were some differences, however: For instance, the Frenchman had not fallen in love with and nearly married his half-sister. In that regard, Dorian felt he had lived a less fortunate life than Alphonse, and that the anonymous author had flawed the work by not including such an experience in the Parisian's repertoire of indecency. Another point in which Dorian and Alphonse lacked common ground was, of course, where Dorian lacked it with every other mortal: Alphonse, like all men who do not die young, died a slow death over many agonizing years. He developed a dread of mirrors. The polished metal surfaces, the pure, still water—all that were once his echo of solace and source of contentment became grotesque objects of horror. He became shriveled. His cock malfunctioned. By the end of his story, the only women who would endure him were worn-out whores and thieving gypsies out for a swindle, their crotches fetid with disease.

It was with an almost cruel joy that Dorian read this latter part of the book, and wonder, with a rosy tinge in his ever-young cheeks. What a different ending the book would have had, should Alphonse have lived Dorian's immortal youth! Perhaps the book would never have had to end, with no moral of the story ever dispensed. Dorian would live the life that nature had mangled for Alphonse Gris. His beauty would never leave him, and so neither would women.

His hunts for sexual release became nightly excursions. Helen remained a vital accessory to his crimes, but she partook less and less in the actual events throughout the years. The last relics of fresh-faced beauty fell away from her like wilted petals. She passed 40, then 45. Her thick, lustrous lips were puckered by wrinkles, as were her wise eyes so many shades of an autumn forest. Her wicked smile was all the more wicked with the leftover lines of laughter, but it was no longer seductive. Dorian was often repulsed to think of engaging with her in any fleshy activities. There were moments in the back of hansoms and along the poorly lit corridors of theaters where she silently asked him for romance. Embarrassed for her, he pretended not to read her subtlety.

Lord Henry Wotton got even older and soon sick
and sooner, it seemed, dead. Helen inherited the obscene
wealth she'd long been dipping into, and she and Dorian
traveled Europe. Together they baited, hooked, and reeled
in women of all flavors. Unless thoroughly drugged, most
of them had interest only in being fucked by Dorian. In
these instances, Helen would, as she had years ago in the
dim dressing room of Sybil Vane, slump against a wall in
quiet voyeurism, to rub herself into a lonely release.

Dorian and Helen spent a good deal of time in London,
too, indeed, most of their time. But it was a difficult place.
As Dorian maintained the wonderful beauty that had so
fascinated Rosemary Hall, and many others besides her,
evil rumors about his mode of life crept through town
and became the chatter of the clubs. But when a woman
actually saw him, actually was taken in by his world-
engulfing gray eyes, they could not believe anything about
his dishonor. He always had the look of one who had kept
himself unspotted from the world, let alone soiled by its
underbelly. Men who talked grossly of him became silent
when Dorian entered the room. There was something in
the purity of his face that rebuked them. His mere presence
seemed to recall to them the memory of the innocence that
they had tarnished. They wondered how one so charming
and graceful as he could have escaped the stain of an age.

Often, on returning home from one of his long hunts
for all the women he could get (and he could get any of
them), he would creep upstairs to the attic, and stand
with a mirror in front of the portrait that Rosemary had

painted of him, looking back and forth between the evil, aging face on the canvas and the pure, young face that was his own. The very sharpness of the contrast quickened his sense of pleasure. He grew more and more enamored of his own beauty, more and more interested in the corruption of his own soul. He would examine with care, and sometimes with a monstrous and terrible delight, the hideous lines that seared the wrinkling forehead or crawled around the heavy sensual mouth, wondering which were uglier: the signs of sin or the signs of age. He would place his white hands beside the coarse, bloated hands of the picture, and smile. He mocked the misshapen body and the failing limbs as a man mocks an ape in a zoo.

There were moments, indeed, at night, when, lying sleepless in his own delicately scented chamber or in the sordid room of the little, ill-famed tavern near the docks that, under an assumed name and in disguise, it was his habit to frequent, he would think of the ruin he had brought upon his soul. In those moments, he would think vaguely of Rosemary. What had become of her? She'd had some moderate success as a painter—that much he knew from social gatherings. But she was a hermit and was seldom seen by anyone. A few weeks after she'd read Helen's letter on her and Dorian's blood bond, she wrote Dorian a note saying only that she was moving away and would no longer be reachable to either him or Helen. She said she would always love him, and hoped to one day learn to love him as a brother, though she did not foresee such a day, and she prayed he would understand and that God would forgive them. She asked that he pray, too.

When he thought of her, of how he had once made up his mind to grow old with her, he thought of all that could have been had fate not been so twisted as his smile in the painting. The pity that came upon him then was so strong that for brief spells he lost all interest in his hedonistic pursuits. He lay in bed for days, reeking of gin and cigarettes, unable to hide from himself if only for a moment of sleep.

But moments such as these were rare. That curiosity about pleasure that Helen had first stirred in him, as they first sat together in Rosemary's garden, seemed to increase with sexual gratification. The more he knew, the more he desired to know. He had mad sexual hungers that starved the more he fed them.

Yet he was not really reckless, at any rate, in his relations to society. Once or twice every month during the winter, and on each Wednesday evening while the season lasted, he would throw open to the world his beautiful house and have the most celebrated musicians of the day to charm his guests with the wonders of their art. His little dinners, in the settling of which Helen always assisted, were noted as much for the careful selection and placing of those invited as for the exquisite taste shown in the decoration of the table with its subtle, symphonic arrangements of exotic flowers and embroidered cloths and antique plates of gold and silver.

There were many, especially among the very young attendants, who saw, or fancied that they saw, in Dorian Gray the true realization of a type of scholar who possessed all the grace and distinction and manner of a citizen of the world. Young men frittered away their youth trying to be like him. Many lost their brides-to-be to him. He scarfed down their virginity and then tossed them back to their bitter beaus. He was careful to steadily upgrade his guests with London's finest, and youngest, among whom he would casually blend. If ever the question came up as to how he preserved such a youthful glow, Dorian made mention of his gorgeous, tragic mother and let his eyes well up with tears. Helen never asked a thing about it, and seemed to feel she too, was protected by a mystical youth. Certainly, she was not.

Following in the steps of his hero, Alphonse Gris, Dorian invested in obscure devices that, likely designed for torture purposes, were splendid for sexual entertainment. Helen had started the collection on one of her solitary travels to the East—shipping back an oblong metal contraption as grandly tall as he, in which one could be hung upside down or bent into an array of gravity-defying postures. There were cuffs for one's wrists and ankles (though they were challenging to loosen and even more so to unlock), as well as a ball the size of an apple swinging from one of its poles that was best inserted in one's mouth as a gagging tool. In a condemned shop at the base of the Seine, Dorian acquired a pair of silver clamps that he learned to apply to a woman's nipples, as well a rusted trap for catching vermin, which he had professionally polished and had all the time in the world to figure out how to use. There were several objects he was unsure as to how to use sexually but was intrigued by nonetheless. The mysterious juruparis of the Rio Negro Indians, for instance, was fascinating and held great sexual promise. The legend read that that women were not allowed to look at it. There were the earthen jars of the Peruvians that contain the shrill cries of birds, the flutes of human bones from Chile, and the sonorous green jaspers that are found in Peru and give forth a note of singular sweetness.

He added to the collection as frequently as he could, and arranged them in a long latticed room with a gold ceiling and walls of crimson lacquer. Some women started back in fear as soon as he removed their blindfold to reveal the room. Others let him lead them in do as he wished, too drugged or jaded to care. There were a handful of women that enjoyed themselves, at least part of the time, especially when he brought out the silver clamps. These types he kept around for a while, until they wanted more, then, struck by the terrifying thought of his mother's ring sitting in his old Uncle Kelso's house somewhere, he cut them loose for good. It was usually upon such incident that one of his malaises came on where he laid about in discontent for days.

But mostly his was a life brimming with the magnificent realization of sexual indulgences. He fancied himself a kind of hero for embracing what mankind had decried throughout time. Era upon era, men and women had banished their sexual natures, hid them in the light-less basements of their psyches, insistent that they must never be recognized, not even by them. True nature of the erotic senses had never been understood, as Dorian, Helen, and Alphonse well knew, and so such senses had remained savage in the majority of minds. The world had sought to starve sexual thoughts into submission or to kill them. But it had failed.

As Dorian reflected upon man's moving through history, he was haunted by a feeling of loss. Civilization had surrendered so much. However old people were when they perished, they died so young in terms of their sexual understanding! There had been mad, willful rejections, monstrous forms of self-torture and self-denial, whose origin was fear, and whose result was a degradation infinitely more terrible than that fancied degradation from which, in societal ignorance, humans sought to escape. Young people retired to their bed chambers alone, convinced the fear of their bodies was not only well-deserved, but noble. Their passions turned clammy in kempt bed sheets. Vast numbers of women died virgins—and some men, too. Men virgins! That, thought Dorian, easing his own well-milked cock back into his pants, was what was truly upsetting.

CHAPTER XV

It was on the ninth of November, about eleven o'clock, on the eve of his thirty-eighth birthday. He was walking home from Helen's, where he had been dining, and was wrapped in heavy furs, as the night was cold and foggy. At the corner of Grosvenor Square and South Audley Street, a woman passed him in the mist, walking very fast: a little huddle of a human in a gray woolen coat scurrying home. She had a large burlap bag, presumably stocked with groceries, in either hand, balancing herself between their weight. Dorian recognized in himself something he'd long lived without and deemed obsolete: an impulse to help another being.

Dorian walked toward the woman just as a gust of wind sent the hood of her coat flying back. Chestnut hair flecked with silvery strands spilled down her back. Something around Dorian's heart seized up. A strange sense of fear, for which he could not account, came over him. He did and didn't want it to be her. He could save himself some turmoil if it was her. But then there would be the turmoil of never knowing. And a part of him really did want to know. Deeper in that same part of him, he wanted it to be her. He wanted to see what forty years of time on earth had done to her. How had those tremendous blue eyes, always so startled by happiness when they beheld him, become small and dim? How had those lustrous lips, so identical to his own, puckered and chapped? Well, his own portrait could show him that, but nonetheless he wanted the gratification of seeing how she, the girl he'd once dreamed would be his wife, had been twisted by nature, how she had been proven to be his older, oh, his infinitely *older* sister.

The woman felt him coming close behind her and whipped around in fear. She dropped both bags. A sheaf of bright radishes tumbled out onto the pale cobblestone.

"Dorian!" Rosemary gasped.

Suspending the anticipation, Dorian stooped to gather the radishes before looking at her face. Some of the radishes had rolled into the street, which he left well enough alone. He grabbed the intact bushel and held it up to Rosemary, asking silently if she still wanted them. She nodded and opened the bag for him to return them. He snuck a glance at her face—one that was uncensored, while she was still looking down to see if any more items had spilled—and quickly assessed the damage of time. He knew with what shock she would look at him when she saw his face still as smooth and lovely as it had been two decades ago. He wished to conceal the shock in his face when he observed how devastated her looks had become.

"Thank you," she said, securing both bags at her feet. She lifted the burly head of her coat back onto her head, and covered her mouth with her hand, as if she would be less seen if she went unheard.

It wasn't as terrible as it could have been—her face, that was. Her eyes were still as large and radiantly blue as he remembered them and her complexion was still clear and rosy. But there were some problems. Her nose, once small as a button, was not so buttony anymore. It had not grown, Dorian figured, but it did appear bigger. This was likely owed to the fact that her once full, dollish face had deflated. She was but forty years old, and not completely sagging, but her cheeks were hollow and the high, elegant bones beneath protruded like rods.

Dorian kept an impassive gaze upon her while she fidgeted and tittered lightly as he remembered her often doing in his nerve-racking presence. The effect was hardly charming anymore, if not altogether depressing.

"You live around here now?" he asked.

"Ah," she said, thinking hard as she bit her lower lip. Oh, what a saddening performance! No, she wasn't even performing. This was just how she was. Inside, she had not changed much. That was what was so tragic about personalities. They carried on their song no matter the deaths in the band.

"No, I'm just visiting a friend," she answered, finally.

"A dinner party?" he asked, stooping to take the bags. "Let me carry those for you."

"Oh, no!" she said, but he clutched the bags despite her protests.

"Well, all right," she said, biting her lip in fury. "Thank you."

"Lead the way," he said.

Rosemary hesitated. "Actually, I—I was hoping we may go to your place. You still live in this area, yes? Oh, it's as lovely as ever. I should like to live here myself someday."

Dorian laughed.

"Rosemary Hall, do you not want me to know where you live?"

Rosemary blushed. Dorian hissed and had to look away. Women really should not allow themselves embarrassment after a certain age. The physical effects were dismal.

"No, that's not it at all!" she cried. "I just, I've been hearing such wonderful things about the way you've decorated your home and would really just like to take a moment to sit and talk with you."

She looked at the bags in his hands.

"Before the dinner," she said.

"Quite a deal of preparations for another's dinner," said Dorian, lifting the bags with a groan to exaggerate their heaviness. Rosemary laughed, tipping her head back to show her long neck that now showed creases. Dorian cringed.

They walked side by side to his house. Upon certain turns, Rosemary feigned to not know the way, but Dorian could feel that she knew the way as well as he did and guessed that she still made solitary visits to his front garden when she was sure he'd be asleep. She had done that at least once when she was a girl, he knew. He had started suddenly from a dream and as if called by the retreating moon, dashed to the window and saw her standing at the gate before the poppies, a lonely dream shadowing her face.

That was before he'd made love to her. Before he'd fallen in love with her. When he remembered this, he felt inside himself for sadness or nostalgia. There was no such feeling, only a grave satisfaction in knowing he had never been meant to marry a girl who would not always be a girl.

"You seemed to recognize me right away," she said, as they turned onto the path leading to his door.

"In this fog? Why, I can't even recognize Grosvenor Square," he said. "But I had an intuition," he said, then smiled, a piece of him turning cruel in a flash. "Such is the way with family, they say."

Rosemary did not react directly to this remark. She appeared to be cold, and hugged herself, her eyes eagerly on the door.

Dorian paused with the latchkey in hand.

"I'd be charmed to have you in, but won't you miss your dinner party?" he said.

Rosemary shook her head. Her teeth chattered. He remembered how, long ago, they'd clumsily grazed his cock. They must be yellowed and jagged by now.

"No, please, let us go in," she said. "I shan't take much of your time."

Dorian chuckled.

"All right, then. Not to worry, dear, I have all the time in the world." He opened the door for her. She went in with some unease, checking to be sure he was following her, but also keeping a distance ahead of him.

"Go along, or the fog will get into the house," he said. "And mind you don't talk about anything serious. Nothing is serious nowadays. At least nothing should be."

Dorian set her bags in the foyer and proceeded to the library where there was a bright fire blazing in the large open hearth. The lamps were lit, and an open spirit case stood, with some siphons of soda water and large cut-glass tumblers, on a little marqueterie table. Rosemary sat in a velvet armchair that Dorian had recently acquired in a lightless seaside boutique in Odessa. It came with two matching fuchsia horns that one could place in the centers of the chair for a most indecent insertion. Presently, the horns were under the chair.

"My servants make me quite at home, Rosemary," said Dorian, pouring them each a glass of brandy and soda water. "I have more than just the Frenchman now, though I keep him around out of pity, and because it can be entertaining to watch an old man try to keep up with those so much younger."

"Victor is still here?" asked Rosemary. She appeared to be uncomfortable in the chair, seemingly unable to decide whether she would recline fully or stay stiffly on the edge. Dorian sat in the opposing chair, watching her. Her discomfort intensified under his gaze. He drank greedily, and was beginning to get ideas. He thought to bring out the horns, imagining the horror on Rosemary's failing face, the cry from her creased throat.

"Indeed. I never liked him much, but I have nothing to complain about. He is really very devoted to me. I imagine he will be quite sorry to leave me when he dies."

Rosemary's eyes widened, then blinked to process what he'd said. Dorian smiled and finished his drink in a gulp.

"Have another brandy and soda?" he offered. "Or would you like gin and seltzer? I always take gin and seltzer myself. There is sure to be some in the next room."

Rosemary raised her glass to show that it was still full.

"Ah, such a lady," he said. "I never had the pleasure of getting you drunk."

He went to refill his own glass and took a long sip at the table before turning back to Rosemary. Her brow was furrowed and she was biting her lower lip.

"Oh, the horrors of time" Dorian could not help but utter. He never would have been able to be married to a forty-year-old. Never!

"Dorian," began Rosemary, sitting forward, her face serious, a welcome respite from all that schoolgirl blushing. "It is entirely for your own sake that I am speaking," she said. "I should want to know if it were me. Anyhow, I think it right that you should know that the most dreadful things are being said about you in London."

Dorian polished off his second glass, refilled it, and returned to his seat. He himself could not help wondering at the calm of his demeanor and for a moment felt keenly the terrible pleasure of a double life.

"I don't wish to know anything about what is being said about me," he said, burping. "I love scandals about other people, but scandals about myself don't interest me. They have not got the charm of novelty."

"They must interest you, Dorian," said Rosemary. "Every gentleman is interested in his good name. You don't want people to talk of you as something vile and degraded—as a man who steals and defiles young women. Of course, you have your position, and your wealth, and all that kind of thing. But position and wealth are not everything. Mind you, I don't believe these rumors at all. At least, I can't believe them when I see you. Sin is a thing that writes itself across a man's face. It cannot be concealed. As a painter, I know that all too well. If a wretched man has a vice, it shows itself in the lines of his mouth, the droop of his eyelids, the molding of his hands even. Dorian, with your pure, bright, innocent face and your marvelous untroubled youth, I can't believe anything against you."

She looked down at her own pruned and spotted hands. "I have seen pictures of you in the paper—at benefits and the like. I've never understood how you've maintained your beauty." She looked at him desperately, her eyes welling. "But you have, Dorian. You are still so beautiful." She broke into a sob. "I never married because . . ." She held her hands over her sniffling nose—how had that ever been adorable?

"Because you are some kind of angel," she went on, pausing to swallow her tears. "My mother's angel," she finished in a hush.

She dabbed her eyes with her wrist and sat back in the chair. She seemed at last able to relax. It was as Helen had once said: Women were all laced up and corseted, crushed up and imprisoned in themselves—until they started crying. Then they unraveled everywhere, utterly adrift from themselves, only to be spooled back together by the poor fools who loved them. A bitter laugh of mockery broke from Dorian's lips.

"Your mother's angel?" he cried. "*My* mother's angel?"

Rosemary looked at him with disbelief.

"Dorian, why do you mock me? I see your soul plain as day on your face. The tainted voice that comes from that lovely mouth so violently contradicts it."

Dorian, now well into the first phase of drunkenness, experienced a sense of clarion rage. It rang in his ears, dilated in his eyes. As he continued to drink, the rage grew louder, and clearer. Rosemary Hall would bear the brunt of it.

Slamming his glass on the floor, he leaped up and crossed over to her. She cried out and lurched back in the chair, holding her glass before her face as if it would shield her. He knocked it out of her hands. It rolled down the chair, its brown liquid sponged up by the velvet, then crashed to the floor in a twinkling shatter.

"You think you see my soul!" he cried. "I can show you my soul. Do you really want to see it? The thing you call my soul?"

A twisted flash of pain shot across Rosemary's face. She started up from the chair, turning almost white from fear. She sucked back a sob, looking around her as if considering exit points, then returned her eyes to him. They emitted a spinsterly destitution, and Dorian wanted to strangle her if only to destroy that pathetic look.

"Yes," she answered meekly, and then in a larger voice. "Yes!"

"Then come with me," he said, extending a hand for her.

She looked at it with hesitation, then said, "But only God can do that."

Dorian laughed. There felt to be an orgy of demons in his stomach, tickling him with pronged feathers.

"Only God, Dorian Gray, and Rosemary Hall," replied Dorian. "Come: It is your own handiwork. Why shouldn't you look at it? You can tell the world all about it afterward, if you choose. Nobody would believe you. If they did believe you, they would like me all the better for it. I know the age better than you do, though you will prate about it so tediously. Come, I tell you. You have chattered enough about corruption. Now you shall look at it face-to-face."

There was the madness of pride in every word he uttered. He stamped his foot upon the ground in his boyish, insolent manner. He felt a terrible joy at the thought that someone else was to share his secret, and that the woman who had painted the portrait that was the origin of all his shame was to be burdened for the rest of her life with the hideous memory of what she had done. *"That awful thing, a woman's memory!"* as Helen had once said.

Rosemary gave him her hand—a dry, old pigeon of a thing—and he led her up the spiral staircase and down the hall. Her hand squeezed his as they approached the landing below the attic. She wanted some comfort, or some intimacy. Dorian felt nauseous. He shook her loose and felt better at once.

CHAPTER XVI

Dorian went up first, a lamp in hand. Rosemary followed closely behind him. She could hear her heart like it was a clock in her brain, wildly ticking with each ascending step. Though Dorian was every bit as beautiful and boyish-looking as she had remembered, more beautiful even than in the dreams of him that had haunted her for decades, he was unrecognizable in character. There was a fearsome scorn in his every word and movement. Rosemary felt that some of the change in him was her fault. *If I weren't his sister, we would have spent all these years in happiness. We would have a flock of pure blond and chestnut children. And maybe even a few hounds.*

Dorian set the lamp down on the floor. The light shot up for a moment in a flame of murky orange, casting fantastic shadows on the walls. The room looked as if it had not been lived in for years. A faded Flemish tapestry, a looming curtained picture, an old Italian cassone, and an almost empty bookcase—that was all that it seemed to contain, besides a chair and a table. The whole place was covered in dust, and there was a damp odor of mildew.

The only sign of life was contained in a gray mouse that sprinted weakly across the room and then was gone through a hole in the wall. A rising wind rattled a hidden window like a cage.

"You insist on knowing, Rosemary?" Dorian asked in a low voice.

"Yes," she said. *My, he really was drawing this all out.* Was there some sexual surprise in store for her?

"I am delighted," Dorian answered, smiling deviously. "You are the one person in the world who is entitled to know everything about me. You have had more to do with my life than you think."

Rosemary felt herself blushing. She bit her lower lip.

"Argh!" yelled Dorian, and turned away.

Was the temptation too much for him, still, after all this time? She couldn't help but think, when she'd been sitting across from him in the library moments ago, as he was eyeing her with such intensity and throwing back brandy, that he was struggling with blasphemous lust for her. She wondered if he had not taken her up to this room to make forbidden love to her—if the attic setting was a kind of negotiation, following a kind of Helen Wotton logic that if they performed their sin in a secret place, it would be as if it never happened.

Dorian paced in front of the covered picture and ran his hands through his hair. He seemed tense, as if he could restrain his desire no longer. Rosemary felt she was the only person in the world who could understand him. She knew the desire so well—had lived pinned beneath it every night since she left his house nearly twenty years ago. That last day had stuck in her memory like a shard of glass. Every experience hitherto walked over it and tore open its feet, unable to walk on. It was impossible to recover from it and she remembered everything not as if it were yesterday, but as if it were that very day. She could still feel Helen's horrific letter trembling in her hands, could still feel Dorian's seed clung to a coil of hair in her nether region. That clump of him had stayed on her for days until she finally worked up the nerve to cleanse herself. That bath had been the last time she had wakefully touched herself, and there had been no pleasure in it. It was just to remove the seed from her. All nights were torment, loaded with dreams of Dorian. She felt his tongue sliding down her navel, down to her most special part, circling there in deft concentration. Days were almost worse, for the daydreams never took her away from her mind, as the night ones did. But at least the days she had been able to paint her way through. Some days she'd painted herself out of altogether. And when she couldn't paint, she prayed.

"So you think that it is only God who sees the soul, Rosemary?" challenged Dorian. He set a hand on the cloaked frame.

Rosemary did not know how to respond. She kept her upper teeth firmly on her lower lip, watching Dorian.

"Ah, stop biting your lower lip, it is driving me insane!" he cried.

Rosemary released her lip. Yes, she still had some hold on him—that was evident by his wild reaction.

"I am sorry," she said. Thinking about his God question, she replied, "Yes, only God can see the soul. Dorian, everyone knows that."

Dorian laughed. His laugh, too, was nothing like the laugh she recalled. It was as if he were badly playing a part, bereft of any human suffering or joy.

"Draw that curtain back, and you will see my soul," he said.

Rosemary looked back between him and the curtain. Was this all part of an elegant seduction?

"Dorian, what is this about?" she asked.

"You won't lift the curtain?" he cried, eyeing her spitefully. "Then I must do it myself," he said. He tore the purple curtain from its rod and flung it on the ground.

Rosemary went numb. There was her heart again, winding up in her ears, about to run out. She heard herself cry out in horror as she saw in the dim light the hideous face on the canvas grinning at her.

"Good heavens!" she cried.

She seized the lamp, and held it to the picture. In the left hand corner were her own initials in her signature vermilion. But no: It was some foul parody, some ignoble satire. She had never done that—would never do something like that. It was why she refused to paint ugly people! But there was no denying that it was her own picture. She knew it, and she felt as if her blood had changed in a moment from fire to sluggish ice.

The horror, whatever it was, had not yet entirely spoiled Dorian Gray's marvelous beauty. There was still some gold in the thinning hair and some scarlet on the sensual mouth. The sodden eyes had kept something of their gray loveliness; the noble curves had not yet completely passed away from chiseled nostrils and white throat.

"What does this mean?" she cried.

"Ah," said Dorian, circling her and the portrait. "Years ago, when I was a boy, you met me, flattered me, and taught me to be vain of my good looks. One day, you introduced me to a friend of yours, Helen Wotton. She explained to me the wonder of youth, and you finished a portrait of me that revealed to me the wonder of beauty. In a mad moment that even now I don't know whether I regret or not, I made a wish—perhaps you would call it a prayer. . . ."

"I remember it!" cried Rosemary. "Oh, how well I remember it! But this is impossible." She looked around the room, desperate for an answer, however ludicrous. "The room is damp. Mildew has got into the canvas," she said. "Or the paints I used had some wretched mineral poison in them! No, this is impossible!"

"Ah, what is impossible?" murmured Dorian, coming close to her and taking the lamp from her.

"There was nothing evil in it, nothing shameful!" she cried. "You were to me such an ideal as I shall never meet again. This is the face of evil."

"It is the face of my soul," said Dorian.

"Christ! What a thing I must have worshipped! It has the eyes of a devil."

"Each of us has Heaven and Hell in him, Rosemary!" cried Dorian with a wild gesture of despair.

"My God! If it is true," she exclaimed. "And this is what you have done with your life, why, you must be worse even than those who talk against you fancy you to be!" She whisked the lamp from him and held it once more to the canvas, taking in all its foulness and horror. The leprosies of sin were slowly eating the thing away. The man depicted looked much older than thirty-eight.

Her hand shook, and the candle fell from its socket on the floor and lay there sputtering. Dorian placed his foot on it and put it out. Rosemary flung herself into the rickety chair that was standing by the table and buried her face in her hands.

"Good God, Dorian, what a lesson! What an awful lesson!"

She sobbed, holding her hands over her face. Then, realizing they were hands that had been puppet-mastered by some satanic force, she began wringing them wildly. Wait, no, she needed them to pray. She steepled them and looked up at Dorian.

"Pray, Dorian," she murmured. "*Lead us not into temptation. Forgive us our sins. Wash away our iniquities*," she began. "Let us say that together. The prayer of your pride has been answered. The prayer of your repentance will be answered also. I worshipped you too much. I am punished for it. You worshipped yourself too much. We are both punished."

Dorian stood by the portrait, his eyes dimmed with tears. *That was a good sign*, thought Rosemary. *Tears! There was a human in there yet—a relic God would recognize as his own and save.*

But Dorian did not want to cooperate.

"It is too late," he faltered.

"It is never too late, Dorian!" cried Rosemary. She got off the chair and onto her knees, facing away from the painting.

"Let us kneel down and try if we cannot remember a prayer. Isn't there a verse somewhere: *Though your sins be as scarlet, yet I will make them as white as snow?*"

"Those words mean nothing to me now," said Dorian.

"Hush! Don't say that!" Rosemary begged, her hands still clasped heavenward. "You have done enough evil in your life. My God! Don't you see that accursed thing leering at us?"

Dorian looked at the picture for a while, then giggled, as if it were whispering to him. His eyes veered to the little table and settled upon an object there. He walked past Rosemary to the table and fetched the object. *My, he had gotten strange in his lack of old age.* Rosemary closed her eyes to focus on praying. She estimated she would pray for another ten or fifteen minutes, and then flee, for her beloved was clearly mad. *Go now!* she thought—but, no, she had to at least try and save his soul. Its destruction was partly her doing. Perhaps it was all her doing.

Dorian moved slowly toward her and crouched down at her side.

"Yes," she cried. "Pray with me!"

"Rosemary," he said softly. "Why don't you get up off the floor? It's been too many years since I've seen you."

Rosemary stopped praying. Dorian's tone had changed. He sounded tranquil and tender. She opened her eyes. He was looking at her with that bottomless lust she'd been fantasizing about in such agony all these years. He held her hand and squeezed it. Her thoughts quieted and then muted altogether. She was his again. Black magic, shared blood, decades of sexless seclusion—none of it mattered. As long as he was touching her, everything was exactly as it was meant to be and infinitely good.

He stood her up and kissed her on the mouth, releasing his tongue into her mouth as soon as his lips touched hers. *Oh, yes!* Her tongue awakened and seized his. She pulled him closer by his neck, inhaling him. With one hand, he grabbed both of hers and yanked them away. Oh, Dorian Gray still needed to have control over her. She would let him do anything he wanted this time. Just one touch to her and she would explode. She pressed her burning crotch against his thigh and moaned. It was as if she was bursting out of herself, uncorked.

"Oh, Dorian!" she cried, feeling for his sure-to-be bulging cock with her pelvis. She rubbed around but could not find it. He kissed her again.

When she first felt the blade on her back, she thought it was his hand moving to unlace her. But the pressure kept going until it was a weeping pain, bolder than anything she'd ever felt.

"Argh!" she cried, as the knife was yanked out and plunged again into her back. Dorian's lips were still locking hers, and his tongue mirrored the jabbing of the knife. Thick, hot liquid filled her bodice. She fought to break from his kiss, but he was sucking her with tremendous strength, and she was quickly losing hers. Her hands tingled. A coppery rush of blood lunged up her throat and she gagged. Dorian kept kissing her.

He removed the knife once more and dug it into the great vein behind her ear.

Though your sins be as scarlet . . . though your sins be as scarlet . . .

On and on went the first refrain of the prayer. She recognized her mother's voice calling her. It was a warm wind of a voice, a sea of yellow poppies.

CHAPTER XVII

Dorian could hear nothing, but the drip-drip-drip of blood on the threadbare carpet. He used Rosemary's skirt to wipe the knife handle, set the knife on the table, and dragged Rosemary to the seat and propped her up. He remembered how, many years ago, when he was just starting out in the world of lechery, he had sated himself on the actress Sybil Vane, and brought her limp, drugged body to her dressing table. She had been alive, though. Rosemary was most assuredly not. She rather looked alive though, from a certain angle. Were it not for the red, jagged tear in the neck and the clotted black pool that was slowly widening on the table, one would have said that the woman was simply asleep. Dorian left her as she was, returned the curtain to its proper place, and closed up the attic. He had to plan his next move.

In his room, he took a lamp and examined himself in the long mirror. The same: He was perfectly the same. It had occurred to him before that if he killed Rosemary, he might kill the curse of the portrait. But no—he was as boyish and innocent-looking as ever. There was no indication that he had just killed a woman.

No matter how he loathed Rosemary, he had not planned on murdering her. He had just been so overcome with hatred for her. And he felt, as he stood watching her spine shudder in prayer, that she was like an old hound that needed to be put out of her misery. He kept imagining bringing a rock crashing onto her skull. But there were no rocks in the attic. The knife, which he'd brought up years ago to cut some cord and forgotten all about, gleamed and glistened as if to sing of its brutal fate on the desk. Ah! He just wanted an end to it all. Though, in order to go through with the act, he needed just a touch more inspiration—one final push into total revulsion. That was when he'd had the idea to kiss her. How happily confused she'd been as he stood her up. With what passion she had returned his kiss, blasting him with her dead-flower breath. He'd never been so sickened in all his life.

But now he was a murderer. And unlike the life of a sex maniac, he had no set of instructions on how to proceed, no nefarious yellow book prescribing his actions. Alphonse Gris had never murdered anyone. Well, no, he had murdered a ragged old gypsy who'd stolen money from him, but that was just a drunken incident in an abandoned alley. It was not a life-altering event.

Rosemary Hall was a person whose disappearance would provoke curiosity and questions. And her blood, Dorian realized as he undressed and washed himself, was all over his place. It had managed to soil his every article of clothing. He would have to do a thorough check of his path from the attic in the morning, before the servants awoke. He would burn the clothes then, too. But what would he do with the body? Something would come to him, he was sure. If necessary, he would ask Helen. She knew every type of criminal. Surely one of them would be willing to dispose of a body.

He dressed himself with more than his usual care, giving a good deal of attention to the choice of his necktie and scarf-pin and changing his rings more than once. Normalcy, or the semblance of such, had to be restored at once. He remembered the two bags of grocery items Rosemary had come in with and ran to the foyer to rid of them. Her gray wool coat hung on a hook above them. Dorian took it down and folded it up into as small as bundle as he could manage. As he did so, he felt as if he were folding up all of Rosemary Hall's lonely life. What was left of her was just evidence to be burned. He could do worse than to convert her to ash in the fireplace in the main dining hall, where twenty years ago, she'd fancied the hideous painting would hang in modest glory. It would be fitting if she were laid to rest there. Sort of sweet. Anyway, whatever deviant he hired to remove her corpse would probably turn to fire, too. As he lifted the grocery bags, a lone radish rolled out and rested soundlessly against his shoe. When he saw it, a heaviness lurched in his stomach and knocked against his heart, smacking it into a fit of palpitations. He forced himself to sit and collect himself before carrying on.

When he regained composure he unlocked a secret panel in the stairs' wainscoting—a press in which he kept his own curious disguises, among them a leather loincloth and matching whip, and stashed the bags and the crumpled coat there. He could easily burn them afterward. Then he pulled out his watch. It was two o'clock in the morning. He thought to call on Helen, who slept very little. He believed he could confide in her the night's gruesome event, but when he imagined her mocking voice he got dizzy.

"To cure the soul by means of the senses, and the senses by means of the soul!" How Helen's words rang in his ears! His soul, certainly, was sick to death. Was it true that the senses could cure it? Innocent blood had been spilled. What could atone for that? Ah! For that there was no atonement, but though forgiveness was impossible, forgetfulness was possible still—and he was determined to forget, to stamp the thing out, to crush it as one would crush the adder that had stung him.

Every year—every month, almost—men were hanged in England for what he had done. There had been a madness of murder in the air. Some red star had come too close to the earth. . . . And yet what evidence was there against him? No one had seen Rosemary come in. The servants had left for the night. The only other person in the house was Victor, and he was half-blind and three-quarters deaf. It would be months before any suspicions would be roused. Months!

He felt that if he brooded on what he had done, he would sicken or grow mad. There were sins whose fascination was more in the memory than in the doing of them, strange triumphs that gratified the pride more than the passions and gave to the intellect a quickened sense of joy, greater than any joy they brought, or could ever bring, to the senses. But this was not one of them. It was a thing to be driven out of the mind, to be drugged with poppies, to be strangled lest it might strangle one itself.

He went into the library and poured himself another brandy and soda. Every second, he glanced at the clock. As the minutes went by, he became horribly agitated. At last he got up and began to pace up and down the room in long, stealthy strides. His hands were curiously cold in his pockets.

The suspense became unbearable. Time seemed to him to be crawling with feet of lead, while he was being swept by monstrous winds toward the jagged edge of some black cleft of precipice. He knew what was waiting for him there— saw it, indeed, and, shuddering, crushed with dank hands his burning lids as if he would have robbed the very brain of sight and driven the eyeballs back into their cave. It was useless. The brain had its own food on which it fattened, and the imagination, made grotesque by terror, twisted and distorted as a living thing by pain, danced like some foul puppet on a stand and grinned through moving masks.

He had to destroy the evidence. He had to destroy the painting.

Why had he kept it so long? For a time it had given him pleasure to watch it changing and growing old. Now, thinking of Rosemary dead in the attic, he knew it would only keep him awake at night. It was like a conscience to him. It was what stood before him and true . . . happiness?

No, he wasn't pursuing happiness—only pleasure: the very thing a conscience was designed to prey upon.

He took the lamp from the table and crept back upstairs and toward the attic. The woodwork creaked and seemed to cry out as if in pain. He stopped several times and waited, thinking he heard Victor who had a kind of sixth sense for his master and often knew when he was in distress. No, everything was still. It was merely the sound of his own footsteps. He tried to be quiet when he released the attic stairs, but they groaned and squealed as they came tumbling down. He climbed them quickly and then pulled them up behind him as was his custom.

A misty blue dawn was seeping through the little window behind the shelf, illuminating the ghastly pools of blood. The events of the night crept with silent, bloodstained feet into his brain and reconstructed themselves there with terrible distinctness. He winced at the memory of all that he had suffered, and for a moment the same curious feeling of loathing for Rosemary that had made him kill her came back to him, and he was disgusted all over again. She was still sitting there, unveiled by the light. How horrible that was! Such hideous things were for the darkness, not for the day. As soon as he destroyed the painting, he would have to do something with the body—at least hide it until he had a better plan. The thought of lugging a corpse around left him cold. No matter how evil his soul, a necrophiliac it was not.

He dragged the purple hanging once more from the portrait. A cry of pain and indignation broke from him.

The figure in the painting was doused in blood. It was there on the painted feet, as if the thing had dripped, on the hand that had stabbed Rosemary as well as on the hand that had held her in place. There was even blood gurgling from the wicked smile. Reflexively, Dorian spat.

He ran to the table and took up the knife. As it had killed the painter, so it would kill the painter's work, and all that it had meant. It would kill the past, and when that was dead, Dorian would be free. It would kill this monstrous soul-life and he would be at peace.

He aimed right for the horrible grin and plunged the knife in. He stabbed it again and again, cursing it. Strips of the cloth ripped down as the canvas caved. He was on his third strike when he suddenly lost all strength in his arms. His legs buckled, and he fell backward onto the floor. His muscles were weak and degraded. It was as if they hadn't mustered a movement in years. He wheezed, his lungs failing to inflate. Everything in his body ached. Time slowed like a dying engine, then stopped with a sickly lurch. Dorian caught a glimpse of his own hand waving for something to grasp onto—it was frail and liver-spotted and the skin hung. The stench of a rotting corpse made him gag and up sputtered a globule of blood. He coughed up more. Unable to move his head, the blood rolled back down his face and into his eyes.

CHAPTER XVIII

There was a cry heard, and a crash. The cry was so horrible in its agony that Victor woke and crept out of his room, shaking and pale as bone, but that was rather usual for the old man. Two policemen, who were passing in the square below, stopped and looked up at the great house.

"Whose house is that, constable?" asked the elder of the two.

"Mr. Dorian Gray's, sir."

They looked at each other and sneered.

"Maniac," said one.

"Of the most perverted degree," said the other.

After about a quarter of an hour of searching the grounds for his master, Victor remembered the attic. Though he had never been told so, he had intuited that he was not allowed to go up there. He pretended to know nothing of its existence, for though his master spent more and more time up there, he was mysterious about it and it seemed to contain some unpleasantries. Every time he came down from a visit there, he was pale and uneasy, and his mood was especially foul. It was haunted by some evil memory, thought Victor.

He lowered the staircase down, hoping the sound of him breaking an unspoken rule would send his master running out to stop him. But everything was still. Victor sensed something terrible had occurred up there and did not proceed up. He would wait for the other servants to arrive. Or he would go outside and flag a policeman. The local police hated Dorian, and often hung around waiting for a crime of some sort or at least a bit of criminal gossip. The latter they almost always got hold of, for it was nearly every morning some woman was flying out in tears or being carried out unconscious by one of the servants and swiftly deposited into a hansom.

Victor found the two policemen outside and flagged them in.

When the men entered the attic, they found propped against the wall a splendid portrait of Dorian Gray as they had last seen him, in all the wonder of his exquisite youth and beauty. In the corner, propped on a chair, head down, mouth agape, was a middle-aged woman, stabbed to death. Lying on the floor was a dead man, in evening dress, with a knife in his face. He was withered, wrinkled, and loathsome of visage. He was so thin and shriveled that his pants had fallen down. Whoever the man was, his time had come—that much was certain. But the cock's time had not. It stood, full-fleshed, erect as a sword. It was quite a marvelous cock, dead or alive. The policemen were too embarrassed to remark upon it aloud, but each gasped his surprise and swore to himself that he would never think of it again and certainly never utter a word to his wife, who was home safe in bed.

ABOUT THE AUTHOR

NICOLE AUDREY SPECTOR is a writer and editor who lives in Brooklyn with her dog, Netta, and her cat, Fellow. She contributes weekly to the *New Yorker*'s nightlife section, among other publications, and co-runs the Guerilla Lit Reading Series in Manhattan.